THE HOUSEWIFE ASSASSIN'S RECIPES FOR DISASTER

JOSIE BROWN

A BOOK BY

SIGNAL PRESS

Library of Congress Cataloging-in-Publication Data is available upon request

Cover Design by Andrew Brown, ClickTwiceDesign.com

Digital Formatting by Austin Brown, CheapEbookFormatting.com

Trade Paperback ISBN: 978-1-942052-15-9

Hardcover ISBN: 978-1-942052-29-6

V022319

Praise for Josie Brown's Novels

"This is a super sexy and fun read that you shouldn't miss! A kick ass woman that can literally kick ass as well as cook and clean. Donna gives a whole new meaning to "taking out the trash."

 —Mary Jacobs, *Book Hounds Reviews*

"The Housewife Assassin's Handbook by Josie Brown is a fun, sexy and intriguing mystery. Donna Stone is a great heroine —housewives can lead all sorts of double lives, but as an assassin? Who would have seen that one coming? It's a fast-paced read, the gadgets are awesome, and I could just picture Donna fighting off Russian gangsters and skinheads all the while having a pie at home cooling on the windowsill. As a housewife myself, this book was a fantastic escape that had me dreaming "if only" the whole way through. The book doesn't take itself too seriously, which makes for the perfect combination of mystery and humour."

 —*Curled Up with a Good Book and a Cup of Tea*

"The Housewife Assassin's Handbook is a hilarious, laugh-out-loud read. Donna is a fantastic character–practical, witty, and kick-ass tough. There's plenty of action–both in and out of the bedroom… I especially love the housekeeping tips at the start of each chapter–each with its own deadly twist! This

book is perfect for relaxing in the bath with after a long day. I can't wait to read the next in the series. Highly Recommended!"

—*CrimeThrillerGirl.com*

"This was an addictive read–gritty but funny at the same time. I ended up reading it in just one evening and couldn't go to sleep until I knew what the outcome would be! It was action-packed and humorous from the start, and that continued throughout, I was pleased to discover that this is the first of a series and look forward to getting my hands on Book Two so I can see where life takes Donna and her family next!"

—*Me, My Books, and I*

"The two halves of Donna's life make sense. As you follow her story, there's no point where you think of her as "Assassin Donna" vs. "Mummy Donna', her attitude to life is even throughout. I really like how well this is done. And as for Jack. I'll have one of those, please?"

—*The Northern Witch's Book Blog*

Novels in The Housewife Assassin Series

The Housewife Assassin's Handbook (Book 1)

The Housewife Assassin's Guide to Gracious Killing (Book 2)

The Housewife Assassin's Killer Christmas Tips (Book 3)

The Housewife Assassin's Relationship Survival Guide (Book 4)

The Housewife Assassin's Vacation to Die For (Book 5)

The Housewife Assassin's Recipes for Disaster (Book 6)

The Housewife Assassin's Hollywood Scream Play (Book 7)

The Housewife Assassin's Killer App (Book 8)

The Housewife Assassin's Hostage Hosting Tips (Book 9)

The Housewife Assassin's Garden of Deadly Delights (Book 10)

The Housewife Assassin's Tips for Weddings, Weapons, and Warfare (Book 11)

The Housewife Assassin's Husband Hunting Hints (Book 12)

The Housewife Assassin's Ghost Protocol (Book 13)

The Housewife Assassin's Terrorist TV Guide (Book 14)

The Housewife Assassin's Deadly Dossier (Book 15: The Series Prequel)

The Housewife Assassin's Greatest Hits (Book 16)

The Housewife Assassin's Fourth Estate Sale (Book 17)

The Housewife Assassin's Horrorscope (Book 18)

Strange Bedfellows

It is a truth universally acknowledged that politics is the second oldest profession—and that, sadly, it resembles the oldest profession in too many ways to count on a gentlewoman's properly sheathed pinkies and toes.

Being the epitome of reticence and decorum, she must strive to stay out of politics at all costs—

Unless, heaven forbid, it is necessary to sully herself in the pursuit of liberty·and justice for all.

But before trotting out onto the campaign trail, she must remind herself about the difference between a lady, a whore, and a politician: whereas both the whore and the politician will perform unseemly acts with the strangest of bedfellows for money (in the case of the politician, this is euphemistically called "campaign donations"), neither the lady nor the whore equates money with power because she holds all the power she needs in her dainty (if not always properly sheathed) pinky.

Speaking of strange bedfellows, the culinary combination of chocolate and peanut butter was popularized with the invention of the Reese's Peanut Butter Cup back in 1928. This take on a pie version will have you crossing party lines to get a slice:

Chocolate Peanut Butter Pie (From Courtney Wade, Gillett Pennsylvania)

Ingredients

- 1 crust made from chocolate graham crackers
- 1 1/2 pints vanilla ice cream, softened
- 2 cups creamy peanut butter
- 1 jar of hot fudge
- 1 container of whipped cream

Directions

1. Mix ice cream and peanut butter with mixer on low speed.
2. Pour into pie crust.
3. Freeze 3 hours.
4. Add hot fudge topping. Return to freezer.
5. Serve each piece with whipped cream.

I LAY ON A LARGE TABLE, NAKED EXCEPT FOR THE SUSHI THAT has been placed strategically on and around my body.

It's not a great look, but this doesn't stop three Chinese diplomats (I use the term lightly; in truth, they are spies) from plucking raw fish wrapped in seaweed and rice, while staring at my naughty bits.

One of the city's premiere sushi chefs slices and dices away at his workstation. Because his chef's jacket and hat are insulated, he is oblivious to the cold air blowing in from a block of dry ice below the floorboards, which flows into a tube on the tabletop beneath me.

This is supposed to keep the sushi fresh. Unfortunately, it has also turned my lips blue and numbed my bum. Beneath parsley pasties, my nipples stand at attention, whetting the diners' appetites for hanky-panky, if not nigiri-maki.

I'm in a private penthouse which crowns a sixty-story building on San Francisco's Embarcadero, its stunningly romantic waterfront district. It is owned by one of the diners —Professor Hong Li, whose status as a world-renowned mathematician gives him the prestige he needs to hide in plain sight. My mission has me working undercover as a *nyotaimori*. In Japanese, the term means "female body platter," but it is universally interpreted as "go ahead and cop a feel between bites of your dragon roll."

The dining room's other major attraction is its well-appointed vodka room—a large glass freezer in which hundreds of premium, obscure vodka bottles are stored at 28° Fahrenheit. Forget sake. If the way these guys have been blitzing themselves on the fermented potato juice enjoyed by their comrades to the near west is any indication, international relations with Russia are thawing at North Pole speed.

My geisha-like role demands that I lay here stock-still. I mustn't shiver or move a muscle. This is particularly difficult whenever Li's chopstick grazes a breast on its way to pick up yet another piece of gunkan-maki.

Either he needs lessons on how to hold his utensils, or he presumes I'm on the menu, too.

How do you say, "Be careful what you wish for" in Chinese? Will a jab in the jugular with a chopstick get my point across?

My mission's team leader, Jack Craig, is located in the apartment directly below this suite, where he listens and watches the video bugs smuggled into the suite's various air vents by tiny drones, just last night by our tech operative, Arnie Locklear. Jack must have guessed how annoyed I am with Li because he whispers through my concealed ear bud: "I guess it's a bad pun to warn you to keep your cool."

He's right, of course. My reason for being here has nothing to do with the fantasies of these slobbering men, and everything to do with our country's national security. Through its encryption circumvention project, Bullrun, the NSA learned that Chinese cyber-hackers have somehow pirated the Department of Defense's secure satellite feed for its Middle Eastern battlefield data networks—the heart and soul of its network-centric warfare.

Experts predict the Chinese economy will reach one-hundred-twenty-three trillion dollars by the year 2040—or almost three times that of the entire world's economy a mere decade ago. Now that China is building itself into a consumer nation, it is looking to curry favor with those who can help it with its skyrocketing oil demands—including the Iranians, with whom the old saying "The enemy of my enemy is my friend," is doubly true when it comes to the United States.

The mandate of my employer—a CIA-sanctioned black ops organization that goes by the name of Acme Industries—is to stop the hand-off of this very valuable intel before it leaves the country. But the Chinese are smart enough to go old school in the delivery process: hand-to-hand, as opposed to e-mail or texting.

For the past week, we've been trying to infiltrate Li's sumptuous penthouse suite, to no avail. He has stayed holed up here the whole time. Body guards are posted outside the steel-enforced, double-door entry. Even the maid who cleans the suite has been vetted by the Chinese embassy employees, as are the well-paid escorts who sleep with Professor Li.

The word *sleep* doesn't begin to describe what he does with these unlucky ladies. And the way he eyes me, I've no doubt he wants me to experience his bedside manner first-hand.

Should I be worried? Nah. I don't have time. This dinner was our one and only chance to stop Li's plot. And from the chatter we're hearing in our targets' native language, we realize time is running out. The handoff is supposed to take place at this meeting, but the guest of honor—the person who will be taking it out of the country—has yet to arrive.

I hope he shows up soon. Otherwise, I may be too frozen to stop him.

My only way to answer Jack's warning is to sigh, ever so slightly. When I do, a slice of fatty tuna roll slides off my midriff and onto the table. Professor Li smirks and mutters, *"Zuòwéi tā de dàtuǐ, tā de rǔfáng fēngmǎn. Hǎo yīgè biǎo, dàn wěidà de, dàng zuò'ài. Wǒ jiù zhīdào jīn wǎn shāo hòu, shì ma?"*

The sushi chef in the corner must get the gist of Hong's remark because his eyebrows roll to the ceiling. Abu Nagashahi, Acme's translator on this mission, snickers.

"Don't tell her," Jack and our tech op, Arnie Locklear, warn him in unison.

After a long pause, Abu mumbles, "No kidding."

Oh, *really*? And what nasty little aside could our supposedly diplomatic friend here have said to earn my desire to wring his neck with my frigid fingers?

Whatever it is, he is saved by the gong announcing the visitor we've all been waiting for.

The men leave the table for the private dining suite's reception room. The rooms are separated by a solid glass wall. Despite closing the glass door behind them, the mirrored ceiling and walls allow me to watch along with my mission team as two workmen roll in a large, beautiful black lacquer box. It stands vertically, and has beautiful Chinese characters on the door.

Hong Li snaps his finger at the sushi chef—the universal language for "If you know what's good for you, you'll get the hell out of here."

The man is no fool. He bows slightly and hurries out after the delivery men. The click of the door closing behind him sends a shiver up my spine.

"Stay perfectly still, Donna," Jack murmurs. "It seems they've forgotten you're there.

Easier said than done. The cold is tickling my nose. I hold my breath in the hope that I can keep from sneezing.

A man enters the room. He's in his late thirties, with a full head of long, blond shoulder-length hair. He wears wire-framed glasses over his large brown eyes.

"Arnie, tilt the living room camera down and left, so that our facial recognition software gets a better look at him," Jack whispers. "Donna, you've also got him in your line of sight. Can you turn your head, just a bit to the right?"

I do so, ever so slightly. Thank goodness all eyes are on the stranger, even those of the professor's personal body guard, a hulk I've nicknamed King Kong. At six-foot-three-inches tall and over two-hundred pounds, should the occasion arise, it'll be a challenge for me to take him. I mean, let's face it—it's not like I can hide my Glock under the pickled ginger garnish in my belly button.

If that time comes, failure is not an option—not if I want to walk my children into their new classrooms on the first day of school tomorrow.

Hong Li smiles at the man and gives him a slight bow. His two associates follow suit.

The Chinese spies smirk at the man's hesitant, unsmiling nod in return.

I don't like the feel of this.

"I presume you want to inspect my handiwork?" The man's hushed question comes out in a stutter.

Li tempers his curiosity with a shrug. "Please, do us the honors." His English mimics his guest's Southern inflections.

The stranger purses his lips as he twists the latch on the door of the exquisitely painted box. Inside is a clay figure—an ancient Chinese warrior. With the push of a lever, the platform on which the statue sits rolls out.

His hosts are awed enough to murmur and clap.

"Wow! What exactly is that?" Arnie asks.

"It looks like one of China's ancient terra-cotta warriors of X'ian," Abu answers. "Back in the 1970s, while digging a well, a couple of farmers in the Shaanxi province unearthed a similar clay figurine. When all was said and done, eight-thousand of them were uncovered. They'd been buried in the necropolis of Qin Shi Huang, the first emperor of China. In fact, there's an exhibit of them here, at San Francisco's Asian Art Museum."

"So, how old do you think it is?" Jack wonders.

"Qin ruled around 209 BC, so it's at least that old," Abu responds. "But this one is a replica."

"How do you know?" Jack asks.

"Because it's the spitting image of Xi Jinping, China's current president."

Darned if he's not right.

"Nailed him!" Arnie yells in my ear. "The dude who brought the box is the sculptor, Carolus Duran."

I recognize that name, too. Known as "the Twenty-First Century's Rodin," Duran's works can be seen in many great art institutions, including the National Gallery in Washington, London's National Gallery, and the Met in New York.

"Your president should be quite pleased with the resemblance," Duran declares.

"When will it be delivered?"

Duran glances down at his watch. "In half an hour, it is to be transported via train to the Getty Museum in Los Angeles, along with the rest of the soldiers in the exhibit now at the Asian Art Museum, just in time for the presidential reception tomorrow evening."

"President Xi will be honored to receive such a unique gift from your president." Li's smile is too wide to be genuine. "I presume you've done as I asked?"

Duran nods. "Yes, of course! I've hidden the secret compartment, here." He points under the left arm of the soldier, which is raised slightly from the torso, as if it's holding something. "There is an indentation, here. Press slightly, and it opens, like so."

To prove his point, Duran presses a panel in the armor directly under the soldier's armpit. Apparently he has pushed a spring lock because it appears to fall into the opening that has magically appeared. Duran's hand disappears into the statue as far as his wrist. He shifts it slightly, and then pulls it out. The panel drops back into place, as if the clay has never moved.

"Excellent," Li murmurs. "Now, we shall toast your masterpiece—and the release of your parents from our hospitality in Chengdu."

Duran winces at Li's joke at his expense.

"Arnie, what's he referring to?" Jack asks.

Arnie's research is fast and furious. "Apparently Duran's folks disappeared about a month ago, while on a group tour of China. Chengdu is one of China's largest cities inland—much too rainy and overcast to be a major tourist stop."

"In other words, they were kidnapped as a way to coerce Duran to alter the statue for their needs," Abu surmises.

"I have a bottle of Russo-Baltique, for just this occasion." Li nods at one of his associates, whom I've nicknamed Snapped Fingers because that is exactly what will happen to him the next time his chubby paws grab at anything on me that isn't wrapped in seaweed or rice. I call Li's other toady Poked Eyes, because he seemed mesmerized by my Telly Savalas, and I'd like to alleviate him of that fixation.

"Donna, don't move," Jack warns me.

He's preaching to the choir. I shut my eyes tightly before Snapped Fingers passes me on the way to the vodka room, knowing full well that Jack will warn me if I need to open them again.

"He's found the bottle," Jack whispers. "Okay, he's walking out now … He's gone. You can open your eyes."

Arnie whistles. "That vodka is worth a million and a half dollars. The flask is solid gold, made from old coins from the turn of the last century!"

I watch as Duran adamantly shakes his head at his host's offer. "No, really, I must be getting back. The museum's curator and transportation director are expecting me to deliver the piece as soon as possible."

Li's smile hardens. "We will take care of its delivery."

Duran's eyes open wide. "But—but that would be considered most unconventional! The artist must always be present when our president commissions a welcoming gift, specifically for another head of state—"

Snapped Fingers pours the vodka into two glasses on the sideboard, and then places them on a tray. In no time, he is standing in front of the sculptor.

"They will understand that you've been called away early, to Los Angeles, to meet with your president," Li's tone is gentle, as if he's talking to a child. "No one keeps great men waiting, am I right? Now, let us drink up."

The fear doesn't leave Duran's face, even as he watches Li take one of the glasses. Finally, he takes the other glass from the tray; he raises it to his lips.

I would wager it's a cocktail of succinylcholine—a paralytic agent—and potassium chloride, which stops the heart. As he falls backward, Snapped Fingers is ready to catch him, and ease him onto the floor.

Li takes something from his inside jacket pocket and places it into the statue's hidden compartment.

"That's it—the intel!" Jack declares. "The president won't even know that he's handing it over to President Xi, along with the statue."

"And should word leak out, he'll be disgraced," Abu adds. "His detractors can use it to call for his impeachment, maybe even his resignation—or worse, call him a traitor, and ask that he be tried as such."

Just as Poked Eyes wheels the box out the door, I let loose with a squeak of a sneeze.

"Oh … *hell.*" The dread in Jack's voice tells me all I need to know: That slight movement caught the attention of Hong Li.

He waves at his bodyguard. "Take care of her."

He's out the door, too, with Snapped Fingers on his heels.

I am left with King Kong.

Jack shouts, "Hang on, Donna, I'm on my way."

I'm hanging on, alright—to the far side of the table, which is now the only thing between King Kong and me. It's too wide for him to reach over it, but the platters I throw at him bounce off, like beer caps in a pong game between two drunks.

He tilts the table on its side and rushes towards me, swatting off my kicks as if they're raindrops until he's got me backed up against the wall—really, against the chef's workstation. He grabs one of my legs and jerks it up, so that I'm now flat on the countertop. He has one hand on my throat. He smiles when he sees my eyes grow big at the realization that he's cutting off my oxygen with his broad thumb.

Gasping, I grasp at anything, and come up with a chopstick.

When I jab his eye, he howls and backs off. He hesitates only a second before yanking it out. A torrent of blood pours forth. I'm a mother of two tweens who play sports like kamikazes and their little sister does anything they say on a dare, so granted, I'm no stranger to blood, but this has my lunch climbing into my throat.

King Kong has me cornered in front of the door to the vodka freezer. He's only six feet away and rushing right at me when I throw my last weapon—the chef's Blue Steel Ao-ko Mioroshi Namiuchi knife.

The good news: as it hits his chest, it stops his forward momentum.

The bad news: when he falls over, it's forward—and on top of me.

Even worse news: As I fall backward with him on top of me, the force of our weight pushes open the door to the freezer and propels me into it—

And clicks shut behind me.

I try shoving the door, but it won't open. King Kong's body is, quite literally, a dead weight blocking my only way out.

My situation is dire. I'm naked, I'm freezing, and for once I'm in no mood for a vodka martini.

Despite the fact that the glass wall between me and the dining suite is tempered and thick, I pray I can penetrate it somehow. Shivering, I stalk the room, looking for a way out of my predicament.

My eyes scan the backlit vodka case. Like the antique gold Russo-Baltique, all of the bottles in Hong Li's personal stash are works of art. Belvedere's bottle is encased in a glass bear. The Diva bottle is especially stunning: a clear cylinder with a tube of precious gems in the center.

But neither of those will give me what I need: freedom.

However, a bottle encrusted with diamonds may just do the trick.

There are several here. Oval Vodka's bottle is covered in them, but unfortunately its shape plays off its name. The cask-like Alizé Vodka bottle is studded with pink crystals. I slam it against the edge of the table, and most of the crystals fall to the floor, so that's of no help.

The next bottle I grab—a brand called Iordanov—is so embellished with diamonds that it glistens in the light. Holding it by its long neck, I once again whack the center table with all my might.

I'm left holding a piece of very expensive glass still encrusted with diamond crystals, where it counts most: around its jagged end.

By now the cold is getting to me. I can barely feel my fingers or toes, and my muscles ache. I drop to my knees against the wall with my homemade glasscutter, which I hold tightly as I etch a square in the glass. Here's hoping it's large enough for me to fit through, and that it's not just the size I wish I were. (Note to self: pinch that inch, then get rid of it for good.)

I don't have much strength, but still, I kick at the etched square. I hear it give way—

Then I pass out.

IN MY DREAM, I'M TREADING WATER IN A STEAMING LAKE. MY children Mary, Jeff, and Trisha paddle toward me. They welcome me with warm kisses, then they swim just out of reach. I shout for them to wait for me. Try as I might, I can't move my hands or feet to follow, but rather I bob and float, dead-man style, with my head just slightly above the water line. Their way of cajoling me to follow is to promise to bring home great grades and be the best-behaved students in their classrooms this year.

In the distance, Jack shouts at me, too. It's hard to make out what he's saying because my teeth are chattering and the hot water is running, but it's something to the effect of *Abu she's coming to, so turn the heat all the way up in the bedroom* and *Donna can you hear me* and *Tell Arnie to stay on Li's tail* and *Donna, I love you, please don't die on me.*

"I won't, I promise. I love you, too, Jack." Did I say that out loud? Am I smiling? If not, then why do my lips hurt so much?

He must have heard me because I feel him slapping my face as he lifts me out of this nice warm bath. Still, I push his hand away because the air is chilly. But he picks me up anyway, and I'm too weak to fight him off. The next thing I feel are his hot tears on my cheek. My own tears glaze my eyes, but at least they no longer sting.

As he kisses them off my face, one of my eyelids flutters open, and I'm staring into the deep green eyes of the love of my life. There is so much I want to say—that I'm glad he got to me in time. That I never doubted he would.

And that I will never leave him, ever, even if it means haunting him for the rest of his life.

But of course, he knows this—which, is why, when I mutter, "What took you so long?" he covers his sigh of relief with a laugh.

He swaddles me in a large terry robe and lays me on the bed. "Taking down the guards was the easy part. It was the damn steel door that took a bit of finagling. We finally cut it open with one of Arnie's new toys—a laser taser. It cut through the freezer wall, too. Good thing, because we never could have moved Li's behemoth of a bodyguard." He warms my fingers between his hands, then kisses each, gently.

"No mission is ever simple." I lick my lips into a smile. I wonder if they're still blue. "Jack, do we still have a lead on the statue?"

"Yes, but we've got some ground to cover. It took us almost an hour to relieve Li's guards of their duty, shall we say. In the meantime, Arnie followed Li and the box. It's been loaded onto an Amtrak Coast Starlight, along with the rest of the terra-cotta soldiers from the Asian Art Museum. They're already on their way to the Getty, for POTUS's private reception with Xi Jinping."

I slide off the bed. When I try to stand up, my legs fold under me, like a newborn colt's.

Jack grabs me by the waist. "Steady, doll. Seriously, Donna, maybe you should sit this one out."

I shake my head. "Are you kidding? And miss my chance to save POTUS's reputation? No way. Besides, who looks more fetching in chest candy, you or me?"

"At this point, anything you wear—including a robe— would be an improvement."

Point well taken. I tie the robe demurely around my waist. "You need me to positively ID Li, and anyone else who may be obstructing the mission. We both know that.

However, after what I've been through, I'll be glad to let you do the heavy lifting."

He shrugs. "My thoughts exactly." He tosses me a black bodysuit, along with a wig, glasses, and a jacket. "If we hurry, we can catch the train before it reaches Oxnard."

Not the most romantic invitation, but hey, I've had worse.

Apparently when Jack said we were to "catch the train," he really meant it. Acme's pilot, George Taylor, flies us into Oxnard Airport. From there, Abu drives us about thirteen miles north—on the portion of US 1 that is called Old Rincon Highway, which runs parallel to the elevated tracks, a place where the two are separated by just fifty feet.

Finally we veer into a small underpass just below the tracks.

Jack looks at his watch. "The train should be coming through in another ten minutes. It's only going about twenty-three miles an hour. At that speed, we'll hoist ourselves onto the car easily by shooting these guns,"—he pulls out an odd looking pistol—"which hold a retractable magnet tether, attached to your vest. Once you reel in the tether, the force of the magnetic suctions on your hand and foot gear will keep us on the car until we can reach the back door. Then you'll break the lock with your laser taser, find the right statue, and grab the thumb drive. You'll replace it with this one"—he tosses me a black thumb drive, and pockets an identical one —"which is filled with enough believable disinformation to satisfy our Chinese friends. Abu will shadow alongside, in the van, for as long as he's got blacktop—at the most, five miles. But then the road disappears and the tracks are hugging a cliff along the Pacific. The next stop is Oxnard, so worst case scenario, we hang on until then."

I give him a thumbs-up. "I get it—a fast in-and-out."

He nods. "Abu will pick us up." He tosses a duffle bag at me. "You'll find infrared goggles in here, as well as a vest, and magnet-laced gloves and shoes. To secure them, twist slightly to the right. To release, press down and lift up, gently."

I snap the locks on my right shoe then I test the magnet on the van's metal floor. Yep, it holds tight as a gnat's arse. "Do we know which car holds the statue?"

"Arnie saw them being loaded into the last three cars," Abu explains. "Unfortunately, he doesn't know exactly which one holds the Duran statue. Li is on the train, too, with a lady friend. They are in the very last passenger car, which is private, and apparently owned by a Chinese conglomerate. It was hooked onto the train at the very last minute. Arnie has changed into an Amtrak purser's uniform, in case something goes wrong and we need an 'official escort' out of there."

I nod. "So, we'll have to check all three cars for it?"

"Unfortunately, yes. Hopefully, it will still be in its black box, so that we can find it quickly and jump off before it reaches its next stop, the Oxnard Amtrak station," Jack continues. "We've got less than five miles of track to pull this off. Otherwise, we lose our ride back to the plane because the road disappears completely where the track runs along a cliff beside the ocean, before going inland and adjacent to the Pacific Coast Highway."

"Then we should split up," I suggest. "Each of us should take a car. If it isn't in either, the one who finishes first can hit the third car."

"Sounds like a plan."

Now that we're suited up, Jack and I position ourselves in the bushes closest to the track.

"Five minutes to show time," Abu murmurs into our ear buds. In fact, we can hear the train's whistle off in the distance.

A minute later we spot its headlight. I'm relieved to see that Jack is right and it's practically crawling down the track.

We wait as the passenger cars roll by. Finally we count off those containing cargo berths. The last car, just beyond, is the observation deck, which is painted in bright yellow. When the last three cargo berths are just a few seconds from us, Jack touches my arm. "You take the last, and I'll take the middle, okay? We'll rock-paper-scissor for the first. On three, okay? One, two … three!"

He shoots his magnet tether onto the side of middle of the three cars. When I do the same with the last one, I find myself being propelled through the air, like a spider on a wind-whipped tendril of its web.

I land on all fours on the side of the designated car. I reel in the tether and tuck the tether gun into my belt. Then I crawl slowly toward the back of the car, where I'll use the laser taser to cut through the lock on the door.

Quickly, I dart through the rows of the cargo's hull, searching for the black box, but it's not here. Through my video lenses, Abu is double-checking the faces on all the terra-cotta statues, just to make sure I haven't missed it somehow, but no.

"Dead end," I shout.

"I've come up empty-handed, too," Jack says. "Since I'm closer, I'm on my way to the next car. Get your exit strategy in place."

I wait and listen for what I hope will be his imminent success. Jack's off-key humming of Keith Urban's *We Were Us* is supposed to mask the exertion and strain of crawling, carefully and slowly, from one car to the next. If I could, I'd cover my ears because yes, he is that bad. As it is, I'm hanging by a thread, ready to jump from my car.

"Step on it," Abu warns him.

"I hear you," Jack insists. "Okay, I'm in … and … no go."

"Then he has it in the observation car with him. I'm closer, so I'm going to get it."

"I'm right behind you," Jack says.

"I'll be out in a jiffy. Just get ready to jump."

"I like your bravado." Jack is joking. The concern in his voice is heard loud and clear, thanks to the echo inside the cargo area.

I know just how he feels.

～

The call girl is a screamer.

Works for me. She's so loud that I can pick the lock of the observation car without them suspecting anything.

And there's the object of my affection: the black lacquer box. Thank goodness it's in the front of the suite, as opposed to through the arched doorway of the car's bedroom compartment.

The woman has her back to me. As she tightens up on Professor Li, her thighs rise and fall in sync with the rocking train. His eyes are closed and his lips are pursed, as if he's willing himself to hold out as long as possible.

You're paying by the mile, so show her who's boss, dude.

Silent as a ghost, I make my way over to the box. Where was the lever again? Oh yeah, on the right side. I pull it and the doors open, and the statue rolls forward.

I slip my hand under the statue's right armpit and press it gently. *Voilà*, a tiny panel falls in. I slip my hand into it and pull out the thumb drive and put the fake one in its place.

I've just slipped our precious intel into a tiny inside pocket on the back of my jacket when the call girl asks, "Hey, where did she come from?"

I look up to see them both staring at me. Li's eyes narrow as he realizes what I've just done. On the other hand, the call girl shakes her head angrily. "My service didn't say anything about a three-way! That'll cost you extra."

He answers her with a slap that sends her reeling backward on the bed. It takes him only a second to flip her over. A set of handcuffs appear, seemingly out of nowhere.

Wrenching her arms behind her back, he cuffs her wrists together.

"Hey, no one said anything about rough stuff!" Now that she's face down, her pout is muffled by a pillow. "I'm not complaining. I'm just saying I'll have to add it to your tab."

Li isn't listening to her. He's already on his way to me, gun in hand.

I dodge his bullet, which ricochets off the suite's metal wall and slams into a lamp, shattering its base. One of the larger shards flies toward him, nicking him in the neck. He curses in pain. Instinctively, he raises his left hand to staunch the bleeding.

That gives me all the time I need to hit him with a crescent kick, which knocks the gun out of his right hand. It skitters out the open door.

I've gotten as far as the threshold when he tackles me. Despite being face down, I kick furiously.

One of my feet must have hit the mark because he curses me, but still he doesn't let go. Instead, he drags me to the open door. While one hand holds me in a chokehold, the other roams over my body, in search of the pocket that holds the thumb drive. It stops over my left breast, which he squeezes with a smile.

Copping a feel—again?

Totally unacceptable.

I bend my knee to give him a sharp back kick, with my heel, to his groin.

As he doubles over, I knock him out the door.

His scream echoes for several moments. When it's not

followed by the usual thud that accompanies bone meeting metal, I look out the door to see why not.

By now, the train is hugging the edge of the cliff that runs high above the Pacific Ocean. There is no beach, just surf slamming rocks.

The sun has already dipped below the horizon, but there is still enough light for me to see Professor Li's broken body, bobbing in the surf like a buoy.

"Beautiful sunset, isn't it?"

Jack is gazing down at me from the roof.

I smile up at him. "Always is, this time of year."

By the time he has climbed down the rooftop ladder, Li's body has slipped under the choppy surf for the very last time.

The call girl shouts, "Hey, where's the party?"

Jack raises a brow. "Want to introduce me to your friend?"

"Not really," I mutter. Still, I walk over and snap open her cufflinks. "So sorry, but all the fun and games are over. Our host has been permanently detained."

She shrugs as she rubs her wrist. "That'll be an extra thou, for the rough stuff."

"You're kidding, right?"

She gives me a look that implies I'm sorely out of touch with the demands for her stock in trade.

No, I'm just sore. I've been frozen, slammed up against a moving train, and almost choked to death.

I dismiss her with a wave of my hand. "Just put it on his tab, he won't mind."

She's not hearing it. "Sorry, cash only," she growls.

The last thing I need is a witness who can ID me. I peel out the right amount of C-notes and toss them her way.

Through my ear bud, I hear Abu and Arnie laughing raucously.

Jack murmurs, "Boy oh, boy. I can't wait to see Ryan's reaction to Donna's petty cash receipt."

Believe me, I wish I got paid extra for the rough stuff, too.

Maybe I'm in the wrong business.

2

Your Tax Dollars at Work!

There is nothing so gratifying to a voter than to actually see public works projects in progress. Roads, bridges, schools, libraries, parks, planes, tanks, bombs, drones and an NSA hacker or two (or three, or three thousand) are just some of the wonderful things your government purchases with your tax dollars!

Whereas state, county, and municipal ballot measures allow you to vote on whether to proceed with public works projects, wouldn't it be great if you actually chose how and where your tax dollars were spent on national programs?

At the next town hall meeting, go ahead and invite your Congressperson to sponsor such a bill. To encourage him to do so, collect a few hundred signatures of your nearest and dearest friends and neighbors, who feel as you do about the issue.

Then watch as he nods and smiles benignly —

Only to do nothing about it, unless you've tucked a thousand dollars per person, into the envelope with your petition.

Those are the true dollars at work.

Hey, he's also the guy who gives the gun lobby free reign, right? They say karma is a bitch. Maybe someday he'll be her bitch.

In the meantime, here's a school lunch recipe that isn't taxing at all on your time or budget, and is filled with all natural nutrition, too:

Blube-Banana SandMash! (From Anna Maria Ruth, Mill Valley, California)

Ingredients

- 3 Tablespoons Almond Butter
- 3 Tablespoons Honey
- 1 Banana
- 2 Slices of High-Fiber Bread (suggestion: Nature's Pride Nutty Oat contains no nuts, so no allergens.)
- 1 Cup blueberries

Directions

1. First, spread the almond butter on one piece of the bread.
2. Then, sprinkle the blueberries on top, too. Smash them into the almond butter.
3. Next, top with slices of banana

4. Next, on the other piece of bread, spread the honey.

5. Finally, place the honey-covered bread on the banana-blueberry concoction, and cut in half.

6. Serve with carrot slices and apple slices for your student's healthy lunch!

"MARY! WHERE ARE YOU?" OUR DOGS, LASSIE AND RIN TIN Tin, are on my heels, circling like hungry wolves as I rush to the foyer staircase with my eldest daughter's plate, piled high with golden-brown waffles. "You're going to be late for the first day of … high school."

High school. The words stick in my throat.

I still remember my eldest daughter's first day of kinder-garten. I held back my tears until she ran across the threshold into her very first classroom—at least, until I got back to my car, at which point I sobbed over the fact she'd begun a journey of learning, making friends, and growing up.

Part of my sadness was that only one of her parents was there to see her take this very important step. My husband, Carl, was on one of his interminable business trips.

In truth, he was working as an assassin for Acme, before switching sides to the terrorist organization known as the Quorum.

When Mary was starting third grade, he disappeared from our lives permanently. It happened the night we moved into this house. It was also the night I went into labor with Trisha. While in the recovery room, I was told by his boss—now mine, Ryan Clancy—that his car blew up, miles off in the California desert.

Ryan also explained Acme's importance to the CIA and the NSA, Carl was an assassin, not a vice president in the international banking conglomerate, as I'd presumed all these years.

In the meantime, if we were to catch Carl's killers, I was to pretend he hadn't died. In other words I had to lie to the new neighbors about my husband's whereabouts, and fib to our children about why their father was never home for parent-teacher conferences, or soccer games, or ballet recitals.

Talk about an extended business trip.

I also joined Acme. My marksmanship was already topnotch. My killer instincts were driven by the need to avenge my husband's death.

They say you have to watch out for a woman scorned. Let me tell you, a woman in mourning can be just as deadly.

Five years later, Carl Stone reappeared in my life. At least that's what I told everyone. At Ryan's behest, I let another operative pretend to be Carl.

Sure, Jack Craig and Carl had a lot in common. Both were tall, dark and handsome. Each had deep green eyes and a naughty grin—not to mention a wicked sense of humor.

And yes, both were top assassins.

I tried to hate Jack for even presuming he could take Carl's place—at Acme, let alone in my home, and in the lives of me and my children. There was a lot of trial and error before I learned to trust him.

Before I fell in love with him. At the same time, I hated myself for being disloyal to Carl's memory.

Later, I was to learn that my real husband wasn't dead after all; that he had faked his death.

Jack came into our relationship with a skeleton in his closet. In fact, she was size two.

His marriage to a former Romanian gymnast, Valentina Petrescu, ended in her betrayal to him, and his country. Carl stole her heart, while she stole a microdot containing the code which accesses Acme's private directory of agents, double agents and assets throughout the world.

We caught Carl. He had a trial in Guantánamo which ended with a death sentence.

But he got away—inadvertently, with my help.

I made it my mission to bring him back in.

Instead, I took him out.

At least, that's the assumption. His body was never found, but it is presumed that Carl now sleeps with the fishes, in Cabo San Lucas Bay.

After all these relationship tests, Jack and I are still a couple. We survived the worst test of all: ex-spouses who have betrayed us and our country.

Is life now normal for the Family Stone? Every day, I pray this is the case. If my children have to deal with life's calamities, I hope it is of their own making, not mine, or any terrorist group.

For Mary, adulthood is just a few years off. As she moves

through life, the lessons only get tougher—including the one that the people she meets along the way aren't always who they seem, at first.

Not only is today a red letter day for her, but for her younger sister as well. Six-year-old Trisha starts first grade. Add my rambunctious ten-going-on-eleven year-old son Jeff to the mix, and what do you have?

A rapidly aging suburban mother, that's what.

I catch my image in the foyer mirror, and I freeze. Oh. My. God. Is that a *gray hair*?

I take a step closer. As I reach up to touch my hair, the slight jiggle of the flesh on my upper arm makes me shudder, and I glance away—

But then I notice my forehead. *Hell, I look like a Shar-Pei.* Make that an old raccoon, what with all the black under my eyes. And let's face it, there's no hiding the fact that my breasts are less perky than I remember.

As I straighten my shoulders, my hand tilts ever so slightly--

Just enough so that the waffles fall off the plate. Rin Tin Tin catches one in mid-air, while Lassie, ever the lady, waits until the second one lands on the floor before snatching it between her teeth and running off with it.

I shake my head and sigh. Then I yell up the staircase again, "Mary! Now! Pronto!"

"Silly Mommy," Trisha's admonishment comes out with a giggle. "Mary's long gone!"

I turn to see her and Jeff staring at me from the kitchen. Trisha was up early today, almost at the break of dawn.

She couldn't wait to put on her new first-day-of-school dress, which she picked out herself. She's also wearing new Mary Janes and lacy new socklets. She slept with her new little Wonder Woman lunchbox beside her pillow. Even now, she has the matching back pack strapped behind her.

Jeff, through a mouthful of waffles mumbles, "Mary asked Dad to drive her in early. They took his car."

But of course she'd rather show up in Jack's red hot Lamborghini. The last thing Mary wants is to be seen pulling up to Hilldale High in a mommy mobile with her kid brother and baby sister in tow.

I can't say I blame her. It's a big day for her. High school is a time when teens exert their independence, experiment—

Get into all sorts of trouble.

Notes to self:

1. Monitor all of Mary's cell phone calls, texts, e-mails and social networking communications.
2. Track her via cell GPS.
3. Do background checks on all new friends, both female and male.
4. Introduce myself–with a choke-hold, if need be–to any new crushes with wandering hands.

Then I remember Jack has taught Mary a few self defense moves, just in case she finds herself in a situation she can't handle.

But that's my point exactly. Will she *want* to use them?

I can't think about that now. Instead, I load my two youngest into my Honda minivan, pronto.

My first stop is Cheever Bing's house. So that I can walk Trisha into her first day of real school, Penelope agreed to let Jeff ride in with her and Cheever.

When we pull up to the curb, she's waiting for us with her arms crossed at her chest. "My God, I thought you'd never get here! Tiffy and Hayley are already at Hilldale Middle. They've been waiting for me for a whole fifteen minutes!" She practically lifts Jeff up by his collar and tosses him into the car beside Cheever and Morton, who are smacking each other as if they're the main attraction in a Punch-and-Judy booth.

As she peels out of her driveway, she shouts, "We've got a big surprise for the whole PTA, so for once in your life, Donna, try to be on time for this afternoon's meet-and-greet."

The First Day Meet-and-Greet is one of the school functions under Penelope's tutelage as president of the Parent-Teachers Association this year.

Make that *every* year. She has turned the position into her own banana republic, and by that I don't mean attendees wear retro-posh attire. Her dictatorship skills are second to none. Just ask any of the mothers who have tried to wheedle out of the volunteer chore she's assigned to them for the coming year—me included.

I can't even imagine what she'll have me doing. Hopefully something that can be contained to, at most, a few hours a month, and preferably at home. She seems to forget I have "a part-time job." She thinks I sell Rave-On Cosmetics door-to-door.

If she knew the truth, she'd probably never let her "darling little Cheever" play with Jeff …

Wow. I never thought about that! Talk about the one thing that would keep her out of my way, once and for all—

Nah. It wouldn't scare her off. In fact, it would make me the first person she'd reach out to when she wants to order a hit—something I know she'd consider in a second, for anyone who's crossed her.

Come to think about it, whatever happened to the neighbor who complained that her magnolia tree was dropping leaves all over his yard? No one has seen him in ages …

Hmmm. I guess the local cops should be alerted that there may be a body buried in his yard—

Or in hers—under the perennially-shedding magnolia. Lately, it's looked very healthy.

Being the good citizen that I am, I'll make an anonymous phone call to the police, from one of my untraceable cell phones.

Let the leaves fall where they may.

"WE ARE *SO* HAPPY TO HAVE TRISHA JOIN US THIS YEAR!" MISS Darling, Hilldale Elementary School's principal, is practically beside herself with yet another new student for the first grade class.

Trisha runs into her arms. After receiving a chuck under

the chin and a pat on the head by the principal who could give Glinda the Good Witch a run for her money, Trisha practically floats into her classroom.

I can't say I blame her. Who wouldn't be drawn to her mentor's gossamer smile?

I wish I could be a first grader. I wish I didn't have a care in the world.

I wish I'd had a principal like Miss Darling to take care of my world.

"I don't remember your RSVP to this morning's parent tea-and-talk, but surely you're staying?" Miss Darling asks.

Suddenly I notice that the other parents aren't just dropping off, but parking and walking in.

"Yes! But of course!" In truth, I'd forgotten about it. And I'm due at Acme in less than half an hour, for a new assignment.

"Go ahead and park, then do come and join us in the library. In the meantime, I'll save you a petit four." She smiles sweetly as she glides back inside the school.

"I wouldn't miss it for the world," I promise her.

I mean it, too. The parents streaming around me are experiencing the same sort of hope and anticipation. Soon I'll be taking tea with my child's teacher. And watching her make new friends. And meeting their moms.

Perhaps making a few new friends of my own.

Life in the normal lane. Love it.

Not to mention Miss Darling is holding a petit four with my name on it.

I zoom away, knowing that Trisha is in wonderful hands.

Until middle school. Then all hell breaks loose.

Time marches on. The trench-like wrinkles on my forehead are proof of that.

By the time I park and run inside, the library is already teeming with both mothers and fathers.

Every chair is taken, but there is still room against the back wall—

Next to Lee Chiffray, in fact—the new husband to Babette, the mother of Trisha's closest friend, Janie Breck.

Babette's widowed state lasted just a little under a year. Her deceased husband, Jonah, owned a conglomerate that manufactured munitions. Its biggest customer was the United States—at least, that was the assumption. Turns out its foes were being armed by Jonah, too.

While Jonah hosted the Russian president at a stateside peace summit held at Lion's Lair—the palatial mansion he'd built on Hilldale's highest peak—my Acme team was charged with the safety of his guest.

It was suspected that there would be an assassination attempt, and that the shooting was to be an inside job. But we guessed wrong as to who was to be the target.

Jonah was killed—not by the shooter, who held a lifelong vendetta against this cruel, sick man. The assassin was my soon-to-be ex-husband, Carl, because Jonah was about to turn state's evidence and double-cross his partners in the Quorum, an international terrorist organization funded and run by an anonymous group of wealthy men across the globe.

And because they were willing to sell out Carl—the hard man who did the Quorum's dirtiest jobs—he turned on them instead.

Unfortunately, we led Carl to them before we could bring them to justice, let alone find their cache of munitions or any intel on the Quorum's cash stash.

Did Carl take this information with him to his watery grave?

I certainly hope so.

Jack, however, is convinced the Quorum is out there somewhere, licking its wounds and biding its time—

And that somehow Lee Chiffray plays a part in Quorum 2.0.

Lee's investment in Fantasy Island—the locale of our last mission, and one of the Quorum's many shell corporations—is somewhat suspicious. But it was with his help that I was able to save my daughter from a boy who tried to rape her.

So yes, I'm willing to give Lee the benefit of the doubt.

Once, anyway.

Besides, it was Babette who taught Trisha to spell *Quorum.*

If she's dropping us a very big hint, it's time we pick up on it. Jack should, anyway. She's made it quite clear to him that she'd divulge anything to him, if only he'd ask.

Lee waves me over. I'm relieved to see that Babette is nowhere in sight.

"I'm happy to see a friendly and familiar face." He holds out his hand.

I shake it, but he won't let go. At least, not until I acknowledge him with a smile.

I wish I didn't automatically blush as well. To cover up my embarrassment, I ask, "Thank you, although I'm surprised to see you here. I thought Babette was putting Janie into Exbury Academy, the private school?"

He shakes his head. "That was the original game plan, but Janie and I convinced her otherwise. Why pay an outrageous tuition, when Hilldale has such wonderful public schools—especially when they're attended by Janie's closest friend. She insisted she'd only go to 'Trisha's school.'" He grins. "In fact, she threatened to hold her breath until she was black and blue. Of course Babette gave in."

I laugh. "It's certainly cute, the way those two have taken to each other."

"Something tells me they'll share a lifelong friendship." He sounds hopeful.

I don't want to believe he's playing me, but there's always that possibility. All the more reason to shrug off his attempts at cozying up. "I'm surprised Babette didn't want to take Janie into school today," I murmur, "what with it being the first day of school and all."

"She thought it more important to go shopping with her stylist." He grimaces at the thought, then adds, "You see, we've got guests coming to town. You know Babette. Her way of prepping for company is to have an outfit for every occasion."

It's obvious that Babette's selfishness bothers Lee. Granted, their whirlwind courtship and marriage took everyone by surprise, but he's no gold digger. In fact, as Jack's research into Lee has shown, despite Lee's humble beginnings on a Kansas corn farm, the end result of his hard work and business savvy is a personal fortune comparable to the one Jonah left behind.

If it's not the money, what's the true attraction? Certainly not her narcissism, childish jealousies, or her blatant disregard of others.

I guess she's great in bed.

The murmuring crowd hushes as Miss Darling raises her hand for attention. "My, my! Look at this wonderful turnout! Thank you, all, for taking the time to take tea with my staff and me." She opens her arms, as if to embrace the teachers flanking her on both sides. "I want to introduce each and every one of them. First let me welcome Miss McGonagall, who is heading up our first grade. We hope she has a long and fruitful tenure, nurturing Hilldale's youngest and brightest students." The first graders' parents are front and center, and their thunderous applause is a reflection of their proximity to the school's seat of power. "Then there is our second grade teacher, Mr. Fitch—"

And so it goes, with all the teacher introductions. Miss Darling rhapsodizes about an instructor's particular strength—the third grade teacher's love of the physical sciences, say; or the fifth grade teacher's innovative math curriculum. Every school needs a champion like Miss Darling. She knows that the growth of a student has less to do with the bricks and mortar that surround them, and everything to do with teachers and parents who love and nurture them.

After a heartfelt round of applause, a parent in the front row raises her hand. "What a wonderful staff! This year is off to a wonderful start. But I can't help but feel … well, we as a community still have so much work to do with our sweet little school. Take the slate of enrichment programs. I know for a fact it's why so many of my son's friends have chosen private schools instead. For example, Exbury Academy has instructors in French, Chinese and Russian, as well as Spanish."

"And the school's library is the size of the local junior college," a second mother pipes up.

"For that matter, Exbury also has a bus to take the children on field trips. It's hard for working parents to take time off for carpooling," another parent points out.

"They have to work pretty hard to pay Exbury's twenty-thousand-dollar annual tuition," a father mutters in a loud voice.

Nervous laugher crackles through the room, but no one wants to voice the obvious: even posh little Hilldale has become a community of haves and have-nots.

A third mom adds, "Why does St. Jasper's fifth grade basketball team always win every game? Could its world class gym have something to do with that—you know, the one with the leather captain's chairs in terraced rows?"

"It helps that the coach once played at Notre Dame," a father in the fifth row grouses. "He knows how to make those kids take the game seriously. If they lose, it's ten laps around that beautiful new gym."

The next thing you know, the whole place is in an uproar. Yes, the parents love what Miss Darling has done—"with so little," is how they put it. "But Hilldale Elementary is competing with the schools who are stealing away those students who see a more challenging environment ..." and "I love what you've been able to do here, but there is so much still to be done ..."

Miss Darling is under no illusions that she can quiet this crowd with a single raised pinky. Instead, she lets loose with a whistle that could hail a taxi on Fifth Avenue during five o'clock rush hour.

The crowd, mollified, zips their lips.

"Hilldale Elementary is a public school," she reminds us. "We do what we can with the state funds allocated to us, on a per-student basis. My mission is to hire those who are skilled and enthusiastic about your children. Now, if you wish to contribute to our foundation, and earmark your funds for programs you feel will enhance our curriculum—"

"A brilliant idea!" Lee declares.

All eyes turn to him.

Of course, they recognize him, if not from the society pages, then from his profile in *Forbes,* or his *Vanity Fair* cover. And those who hadn't attended the reception welcoming them back from their world tour honeymoon would have read about his marriage to Babette in either the *New York Times'* "Vows" column, or the full-page spread in *Town & Country.*

"I'd be the first to belly up to the bar. I'll make a one-hundred-thousand-dollar donation. In fact, make that a five-dollars-to-one matching grant."

The parents are too stunned to speak. Suddenly, one of them applauds. In no time, everyone is clapping.

Miss Darling murmurs, "That's quite generous of you, Mr. Chiffray. How would you like it earmarked?"

He opens his arms wide, as if embracing the whole room. "I'll leave that up to you—and the parents, of course. The bottom line is that we're all in agreement. Our children deserve a first class—that is, a *world* class—school. Why pay lip service to our ideals? I say put our money where our mouths are. It's a matching grant, so let's think out of the box. Perhaps those who spoke up first would like to chair a committee for this new vision of our community school. You can also mobilize the other parents who couldn't make it here today to do likewise."

Once again, the room is energized. Everyone seems to be talking at once.

Miss Darling walks up to Lee and gives him a hug. "Thank you so much, Mr. Chiffray. We have many wealthy families in Hilldale. They see their children—and their children's schools—as a reflection of their own success. I've done my best not to let them down, but the purse strings are always tight." Miss Darling's worry shows up as a hairline crack in an otherwise perfect porcelain brow.

"Glad to be of service." He hands her a business card. "Here's my private email. Keep me abreast of any major fundraising benchmarks. It will be interesting to see which programs will benefit from it."

I'm already twenty minutes late for my meeting at Acme, so I shake Miss Darling's hand and follow Lee out the door.

"That was quite a speech in there," I say, as I pass him. "The way you won over that crowd, you could run for public office."

"Ha! I may be impulsive, but I'm not crazy." He stops, as if a thought just struck him. "Unless someone offers me the presidency. But they'd have to promise that it's a slam-dunk. I only play to win."

A fellow Acme agent, Dominic Fleming, knows this first hand. During a Fantasy Island baccarat tournament, someone laced his martini with Digitalis, and he went into anaphylactic shock.

Dominic survived, but Lee won the baccarat tournament.

We have no proof he was involved, and I would hate to think it were the case.

But if there's one thing I've learned, it's that things are never as they seem.

For Janie's sake, I hope he's one of the good guys.

3

Political Parties

Organizations that seek to achieve political power by electing its members to public office are called political parties.

Joining such a party is thought to be free. Wrong. As with everything in life, you pay to play.

In this case, it's probably your belief in your party that is claimed as payment, since those in the party who are nominated, run and are elected to public office invariably vote the interests of those who really put them in office: not necessarily you or the rest of their party members, but their largest donors.

You've heard it before and you'll hear it again, here: follow the money.

Please don't call me a party pooper. Instead, consider me your party planner! I'll start by passing along this perfect recipe for your next cocktail party:

Crescent Chicken Rolls (From Melinda Stahnke, Conyers, Georgia)

Ingredients

- 2 cups shredded Chicken
- 1 small onion, diced
- 1 cup cheddar cheese
- 1 can evaporated milk
- 1 can cream of chicken soup
- 2 cans crescent rolls (8 pack)

Directions

1. Preheat oven to 400 degrees and grease a casserole dish.
2. Mix chicken, onion and cheese.
3. Place a small handful on crescent roll, roll it up and place in pan.
4. Fill all the rolls and place in pan, not quite touching.
5. Sprinkle any remaining chicken mixture over rolls.
6. Mix cream of chicken soup and evaporated milk, and pour over the rolls.
7. Bake at 400 degrees for time on crescent roll packaging.

"ABOUT DAMN TIME YOU GOT HERE," JACK MUTTERS TO ME. "Thank goodness Ryan's been on an emergency call for the past half-hour, otherwise he'd have your scalp. What took you so long?"

"First day of school. Parent-Staff meet-and-greet. You know how it is."

I look around the conference room, where my Acme mission team has gathered. Besides Jack, there's Abu Nagashahi, who acts as our cut-out and back-up; Arnie Locklear, our tech op; and Emma Honeycutt, who provides the team its ComInt.

There must be some angle of this mission that includes the Quorum because even Dominic Fleming, Acme's London asset and the new head of Quorum intel, is also here. He and the rest of the team are gathered around a laptop, sitting in the middle of the conference room.

"Everyone looks so engrossed. What have I missed?"

Before Jack can answer, Dominic solemnly beckons me over. "Donna, thank goodness you've come! Your fine eye is badly needed on this."

"Of course, Dominic, any way I can help." Has there been a terrorist attack? The assassination of a head of state? A deadly virus released on an unassuming public?

I grab Jack's arm to nudge him forward, too, but he pulls away. Shaking his head, he declares, "Trust me, this is more your area of expertise than mine."

I'm flattered that he'd admit that. I head over to the laptop to see what has them mesmerized.

Pictured on the screen is a very elegant study. The room's high, coffered ceilings are adorned in Italianate frescoes. Three of the walls are ornately-paneled in an Empire style, whereas the fourth holds a deep-set bookcase. Antique knickknacks—vases, statuettes, photos—are artfully displayed among its books. A set of French doors are open slightly. The thick curtain seems to be moving slightly in the breeze. The desk by the windows is a Louis IV, whereas the sofa flanking the bookcase is neo-Gothic.

Dominic points toward the screen. "Your opinion, please."

Nothing looks out of the ordinary. There is no body on the floor. No bloodstains, or bullet holes.

"*Hmmm.* What exactly are we looking at?"

"The sofa fabric," Dominic says, with all seriousness. "It's a Pierre Frey velvet. Quite frankly, the texture concerns me." With a click of the mouse, he magnifies a piece of the furniture. "At first I thought it would do the trick, but now I'm leaning toward this patterned tapestry"—another click shows the same sofa in the same setting, but this time it's covered in a bird-of-paradise print—"which Abu claims adds needed depth to the room. Emma agrees with him, but Arnie and I are leaning more toward the subtlety of the velvet—"

"Wait—you mean to tell me this is about some old couch you're recovering?"

"My dear, this just isn't 'some old couch.' It's a priceless antique! More to the point, it is to be the focal point of the library in my new little cottage."

"All the more reason to go with something vibrant," Emma declares. "The goal is to make a statement."

"But that particular pattern is too busy," Abu counters. "And you can make the same statement with texture."

"Not to mention the velvet feels more voluptuous," Arnie interjects.

Emma rolls her eyes. "Oh? How would you know?"

Arnie's face turns red. "Well … if you must know, I have a full-body snuggy made from this same material."

Dominic chuckles. "Oh, I doubt that seriously, old boy. This is one-hundred-and-twenty dollars a yard—"

"Enough of this nonsense!" I slam the computer screen shut. "You're arguing over nothing, because Dominic's little hovel has no 'library.' It's only twenty-five hundred square feet."

He looks down at his Patek Philippe watch. "Not as of eight o'clock this morning. The bulldozers are digging out the new west wing, as we speak."

"You're adding a whole wing? That's insane! Dominic, we can't put you up forever!"

Since his transfer per diem ran out, he's been bunking in the bonus room over our garage for over a month now. It wouldn't be so bad if some of Hilldale's yummy mommies hadn't pegged him as the town's DILF du jour. Jack's suggestion is that we put in a revolving door.

I say that the best solution is to kick the bum out, and good riddance.

"Perfection takes time," Dominic sniffs. "My God,

woman, Rome wasn't built in a day. Chateau Fleming won't be either."

"Right now, your 'Chateau Fleming' looks like the ruins of Pompeii. When will the renovation be completed?"

He furrows his brow. "Not to worry, my dear. I've been cracking the whip on my team of master craftsmen. They are working on it, day and night."

I envision such a whip, but in my fantasy, it is cracked over Dominic's backside.

I'm just about to let him know that my next warning will come from a cat-o-nine-tails when Ryan comes bounding into the room. "Glad to see you're all here, and accounted for, people." He nods in my direction, just to let me know that my tardiness was duly noted. I take a chair, and burrow down deep.

"We've got two new clients: the Democratic National Committee and the Republican National Committee. From now until Election Day, we'll be working them in tandem."

Emma raises her hand. "Isn't that a conflict of interest?"

Ryan shakes his head. "In fact, they approached us together. As you know through recent media coverage, as we enter the last few weeks of the primary season, both the Republican and Democratic primary races are running neck-to-neck horse races, with delegates split between three candidates in each party. While choice is great for the American people, the candidates' one-ups-manship and political posturing has hit an all-time high. And now one candidate has refused to accept a Secret Service security detail, claiming it's 'a waste of taxpayer dollars.' Not to look like sissies or spendthrifts on the nation's dime, the other candidates have followed suit."

"So, Acme has been hired to be their private bodyguards?" Jack asks.

Ryan nods. "The NSA has detected a high threat level throughout the primary season, but nowhere higher than right here, in California, where the word 'assassination' appears in every cipher. It's inevitable that several, if not all, of the candidates will be visiting our fair state at least once more prior to the final delegate vote at the conventions, which are just a few weeks away. They're here not only to press some flesh, but to refill their campaign coffers. Keep in mind, one-eighth of all U.S. citizens live in the state. It's also one of the three wealthiest in the nation, what with its key industries: high tech, entertainment, and financial management."

He hits a button that sends a file to our personal iPads. When I click it open, I find dossiers on the now very-familiar candidates in question.

"Not only has Acme assigned a specific team to each candidate, as with other of our metro-based assets, we're sending in your team whenever one of them is on the West Coast," Ryan continues. "You'll be acting as a 'ghost squad,'—that is, working the crowds in plain clothes. Since we don't know if it's an inside job, some of you will be working within the candidate's entourage, while others will be assessing the surrounding area. At all times, you're to think like the shooter."

"Will the candidate know about us?"

"Certainly. One of you will always be in the candidate's inner circle. Only the candidate and one key staffer will know your true function." He clicks the computer screen, and a familiar face appears. "Our first candidate is Senator Franklin Percy. He's due tomorrow by private jet, landing at Long Beach."

"A GOP two-termer hailing from Florida, right?" Jack asks.

Ryan nods. "The very same. The party positions him as a hero during the US invasion of Panama, in '89. Retired Marine Corps Major General. He sits on several Senate committees, including Defense and Finance. As you can imagine, he is a strong hawk."

"What do we know about him, personally?" I ask.

"He's been married to the same woman for thirty years—Addie Franks Percy. They're childless."

"Any known enemies, or possible threats?" Abu asks.

"The other day, an untraceable note was delivered to his house." A photo of the letter appears on the screen. The message is a single line, typed:

You will soon face the consequence of your most shameful act.

"Can't be anymore cryptic than that," I point out. "Does he have any idea what this may refer to?"

"He has faced hecklers on all of his campaign stops. They aren't too happy that he co-wrote the bill that bailed out the banks and mortgage lenders during the home loan crisis. At the same time, now that the rates are rock bottom, he's given little support for homeowners who wish to negotiate a reduced rate, rather than being tossed out of their homes."

"They've got a point," Arnie reasons. "Now that the housing bubble has burst and massive layoffs have taken place in all business sectors, selling your home is almost impossible. To top it off, those who can still purchase homes are finding it hard to qualify. It's a vicious circle."

Ryan nods. "Some of those who are most vocal against Senator Percy are retired vets who were once homeowners, but who now live in their cars." He shifts to Jack. "While he's on our turf, you'll be part of his entourage at all times. You're a few years younger, but your military background aligns with his. He can always introduce you as a former aide, when he was assigned to the Pentagon after active duty."

Jack nods. "What's his itinerary?"

"His first stop is the port of Long Beach, for a photo op with union dock workers. Next he'll head over to the West Los Angeles VA Hospital, for a tour. Afterward, he's speaking at a luncheon at the Sunset Tower, with entertainment media executives. Then he's speaking to UCLA students on the necessity of an aggressive NSA. He'll see reporters for an hour before heading to a private dinner in his honor, held by a banker's trade association."

"His itinerary will certainly keep us on our toes," Dominic murmurs.

"To say the least." Ryan grimaces. "The dossiers have

your covers for each event. Emma will be in a van marked as a press vehicle, which will serve as mission central." He dismisses us with a nod toward the door. "Bring your A game. One of the lives you save will be our next president. If we blow it, Acme won't be the contractor of choice for POTUS or any of the security agencies."

Jack walks me out to my van. "Hey, got time for a quick bite?" I ask.

He starts to nod, but then frowns. "Wish I could, but Dominic still has to debrief me on his trip to London. Apparently our cousins across the pond are also looking into our new neighbor, Mr. Chiffray."

"Really? Why so?"

"Remember Sugar CEO Number 3—the Quorum member you so aptly nicknamed Jabba the Hutt?"

"The food fetishist? I'll never forget him! I've had an aversion to mint jelly ever since." I shiver at the thought of greasing myself up with the stuff, in order to crawl out from under his dead carcass.

Trust me, you had to be there.

"In the twenty-four hours before MI5 could get in there and search the place, Lee purchased Baron McBacon's townhouse on Kensington Palace Gardens then gutted it."

"Maybe he did it as a pre-wedding present for Babette."

"Or maybe he's looking for something he thought the Lord Lard Ass left behind, that may have incriminated him and the rest of Quorum 2.0. In any regard, it's something to put in Mr. Chiffray's much-too-thin dossier."

"As it turns out, I had a Chiffray sighting of my own."

His right brow arches in anticipation.

"Like Trisha, Janie is enrolled in Hilldale Elementary School. And like all good daddies, Lee was there for the first day of school."

"Hey, I would have been there, too, but I had my own carpool duties."

"Yes, so I heard—after the fact." I shrug. "That's okay, I get it. Only one of us gets to be the 'cool parent.'"

"'Cool' is outdated. I'm considered 'wicked.'" He smiles as if to say, *Don't we both know it.* "Other than exchanging longing glances, were you able to get anything out of him?"

"No, but the school did—a half-million dollar donation, as a matching grant." I hop into my car. "An amount that means nothing to someone who can gut a London estate without batting an eye. Can't you just admit that you're wrong about him?"

"Tell you what. If I haven't proven I'm right before Dominic moves into his new abode, I'll acquiesce to your woman's intuition."

"Thanks—for nothing. We both know *that's* going to be a long haul."

"Think you can twist Aunt Phyllis' arm to stay a couple of days with the kids while we babysit the senator?"

"I'll call her the minute Penelope releases me and the other PTA moms from whatever fresh hell she has planned for us." I start my engine. "Oh, and by the way, I'm picking up Mary from school. Jeff is staying after school for basketball practice, but you can grab Trisha at two-thirty. If you're lucky, maybe you'll run into your mystery man.

He's acting so generous perhaps he'll just answer all your questions."

Jack's smile fades. "If it were you asking, I'm sure he would."

I can't tell him that I think he's right. Instead, I hit the road.

4

Spin

A politician's attempt to shape the way the public looks at an issue or event, either through the media or in person, is called "spin" because it is quite similar to how a tennis player directs his balls at his opponents.

Only in this case, the only balls are actually on the politician, and are usually bigger, due to his audacity.

Political advisers who spin for their candidates are known as "spin doctors."

Speaking of spin, the best way to manage the moisture of pizza dough is to toss it. No joke! And not only does spinning the dough help create that round shape, the airflow over the dough's surface dries it out just enough to make it less sticky and easier to handle. In fact, the right amount of airflow makes for a perfectly crispy crust!

How to Toss the Dough

1. As long as your dough is made with yeast, you can use either homemade or store-bought dough. The dough should be room temperature, shaped into a ball, and dusted with flour.
2. Prep your work area with flour. Also, keep a bowl of flour nearby.
3. Press out the dough with your hands to form a disc about 10 inches across and a half-inch thick. Yes, you can use a rolling pin.
4. Pick up the dough and drape it over your hands. One hand should be palm up, the other in a fist.
5. With the palm-up hand, lift and spin the dough into the air. It just needs to be high enough to get a rotation going.
6. Catch the dough on the backs of your fists, which are flatter. Your fingers should always be closed!
7. Repeat until the dough stretches to the desired size, usually around 12 inches.

"LADIES! LADIES! *AT-TEN-ZION-AY*!"

It doesn't surprise me at all that Penelope pronounces this last word as if she were Benito Mussolini. Truth be told, she shares many traits with Italy's former dictator. Elegantly-tailored suits. Love of opera. The ability to strike terror in those she rules over. Were someone to gift Penelope with the nickname, La Douche (English, therefore no accent needed) the reference would be well-taken.

"Everyone, please gather around," she commands. "It's time to dole out this year's volunteer assignments."

Instead, this crowd of middle school mommies shrinks back against the wall, as if she's asked us to line up for the guillotine. We have drunk the Kool-Aid, literally (the melted sherbet and frozen fruit ring made it palatable, but I think vodka would have been more appreciated) and figuratively, demonstrated by the fact that we stand here like lambs going to slaughter.

For their sakes, I hope the elementary school moms have a kinder, gentler, dictator.

"Not to worry, people! This process will be harmless. In fact, this year's theme is 'Let's Have a Blast!'" To prove she means what she says, Penelope motions her sergeants-at-arms—Tiffy Swift and the unfortunately named Hayley Coxhead—to come forward with what looks like a wheel made up of individual spokes.

Put at ease, the other mothers coo and smile again.

Frankly, I think their relief is a bit premature. No matter how Penelope tries to dress things up by writing them on those colorful wheel spokes, the same nasty chores await us.

"When I call your name, you'll come up and spin the wheel. The task it lands on will be yours. If the necessary number of volunteers for an assignment have already been chosen, the spoke will be removed. Fair and square, don't you agree?"

Heads bob solemnly.

I raise my hand. "Wait a minute! What happened to the

old method? You know, we peruse the sign-up sheets and write our names beside the job we want?"

"Too mundane. This is why you're never chosen for the fun, creative tasks, Donna—because you have no sense of adventure," Penelope declares. "Time to spin! And may the odds be ever in your favor!"

Seriously, a *Hunger Games* quote?

I know how to kill with one stab of a wheel spoke. Penelope better hope she doesn't find this out the hard way.

As names are called, the wheel is spun and the number of assignments are whittled down. I wince when I realize that the choice ones are being grabbed up by Penelope's favored few. *Hmmm …*

When my own name is called, I make my way toward the front of the room, where the wheel awaits me. I feel like Dead Mom Walking. The wheel looks innocent enough. A slot or two on the Father-Daughter and Mother-Son dance decoration committees are still up for grabs, as are the once-a-month school field trip, and Scrip tallying positions, so maybe I'll pull something that's easy to do.

I churn the wheel, close my eyes and pray.

"Donna chose 'Lunchroom Lady!'" Tiffy intones.

Hayley smiles viciously. "That's under my supervision."

Noooooo …….

Doling out food, and cleaning up the tables afterward? Not to mention, you have to wear the dreaded hairnet.

I look at the others who have also pulled this suicide mission. Is it a coincidence that two of them shared the Siberia table with me at the Hilldale Women's Club luncheon? These other unlucky winners include all three-hundred pounds of plumpness Lucinda Manley, and Tara Wills, whose fantasy face and figure put her in the sights of Penelope's husband, Peter. She turned him down, but Penelope still blames her for looking like a living Barbie doll.

I bide my time until the last assignment is given. As the other women filter out, I walk up to Penelope. "I'd like to inspect the volunteer wheel."

"I don't know what you're insinuating," Penelope sniffs. The looks she exchanges with Hayley and Tiffy imply otherwise.

I take the wheel anyway. I'll have Arnie give it a once-over. If it's been rigged, he'll figure it out.

Then there will be hell to pay.

Suffice it to say what I can do with a spoke is not something to discuss in polite company.

I PULL UP INTO HILLDALE HIGH'S CARPOOL LANE AT EXACTLY three-thirty. School let out at three o'clock, so I presume the joint should have cleared out enough that Mary, Wendy and Babs won't be too disappointed to go home in my mommy mobile.

I am so wrong.

Three much older boys hover over the girls, who are sitting on a bench by the curb. The tallest of these man-boys leans in toward Mary. One leg is propped up on the arm of the bench. His body language reads, "You're mine."

If he were looking in my direction, my body language might be just as easily read.

And he'd be running for his life.

When Mary sees me screech to the curb, her coy smile disappears. She doesn't know it but I've tapped open a secret panel holding my spare Glock 23.

Only the look of guilt in her eyes keeps me from pulling it out.

I motion toward the park across from the school, indicating that I'll be waiting for her there. She nods slowly, and holds up two fingers.

I nod. Yeah, okay, I'll give you two minutes, and not a second more.

As the car glides past, Mary taps her friends. Reluctantly, they move away from the boys, who wave them off. The girls huddle and whisper as they walk my way. I don't like the way the boys smile knowingly and nudge each other before heading off toward the gym.

I pull over to the curb and the girls hop in, still giddy.

"Good first day?" I ask.

Wendy giggles. "I'll say! Right, Babs?"

Her friend's blush is almost the same shade as her coiling copper locks. "I wouldn't make too much out of it. Everyone knows Blake McAllister is dating Erin Long."

"Well, he must have forgotten it, because he was following you around all day." Mary raises her brows to emphasize the implication.

"Are those boys sophomores?" I ask innocently.

"Well … not exactly, Mrs. Stone," Wendy answers. The other girls smother their snickers.

Actually, I already have my answer. After snapping a picture of the boys with my iPhone, I then tapped into the school's yearbook database. With the help of Acme's facial recognition software app, I've ID'ed them as seniors—and very popular ones, at that.

Too popular, in fact. In their junior year, the boy with his sights on Mary won the title "Biggest Player," while Babs' admirer was voted "Most Handsome."

Every other shot of him in the yearbook shows him entwined with the buxom blonde whom Babs is already quite aware of.

"Babs, Wendy, I'm sure your mothers would feel as I do— that you should take a few months to meet as many people as possible, boys and girls. That way, you have time to test the relationship and establish friendships with those you can trust."

The girls purse their lips to keep from laughing.

Mary sighs. "Mom, you just don't understand."

I turn to her and murmur, "Yes, I understand perfectly."

The tone of my voice warns her not to argue.

Except for the faint honks of other cars' horns emanating through the windows, the rest of the ride is enveloped in a heavy silence.

As I pull into Babs' driveway, Mary turns to her friend. "I forgot to write down the link where our Poli-Sci teacher posts our semester assignments. Can you text it to me?" Her smile is innocent enough, but her wink is anything but.

So far, I'm hating high school.

"When does Aunt Phyllis get here?" Trisha demands. "I want her to help me with my school project." She holds up a large cardboard sheet entitled ALL ABOUT TRISHA.

"Any moment now," I promise. "She said right after dinner, but before bedtime."

I take the board from her. It is divided into six large squares, each labeled with a number from one to six. "What goes into each square?"

"The most specialish things in my life! They are called 'mo-men-toes.'" She savors each syllable, as if doing so is creating a memory, too.

Jack pulls her into his lap. "It'll be hard to tape your teddy bear to cardboard, without it bending."

She chuckles. "I don't need to put *him* up there. I'll find a picture of me holding him, maybe when I was a baby." She kisses Jack on the cheek. "You can help me choose things to put on my board. But I've only got a week to do it, so we have to work quickly."

"It's a deal. I work well under pressure. Ask your mom." He nodss at menods. "We'll begin right after dinner—if it's okay with your mom to break protocol, just this once."

I smile. "Sure, I'll make an exception, just this once. In the meantime, Trisha, why don't you work on your New Words sheet?" Homework around the kitchen table before dinner is a family tradition, no cell phone calls or texting allowed until every assignment is completed. Trisha is as happy as a clam to finally have been initiated into this rite of passage, especially since I'm making her "special-ish" meal of all: meatloaf and rosemary roasted red potatoes.

Not Mary. Yes, she loves my meatloaf, too, but she'd much prefer to be upstairs in her room, so that she can text her friends without my knowledge.

Jeff looks up from the table, where he's working on his math homework. "Hey, can you help me, too? I'm running for class president and I need planks in my platform. So far I've got 'Freedom from Tyranny,' 'Power to the People' and 'Democracy, not Dictatorship.'"

Jack and I look at each other, then back at Jeff.

I smile down at my son. "I'm so proud of you, Jeff. But you do know we live in a democracy, right?"

He scowls. "Not if Cheever wins the election. He'll run our class like a tota … totali …"

"Totalitarian," Jack offers.

"Right! Like a totalitarian regime! Someone's got to stop him, but everyone's afraid of him." He shakes his head. "Not me."

"The nut doesn't fall far from the tree," I mutter.

Jack snorts. "This from the woman who is about to ask Arnie to analyze Penelope's Wheel of Pain."

"My son and I are cut from the same cloth. We like righting wrongs." I tweak Jeff's nose. "I'm so glad I can be an inspiration to you."

"That's what you think," Mary murmurs just loud

enough for me to hear. She turns to Jeff. Feigning innocence, she asks, "Hey, who's teaching Civics this year?"

"Miss Bliss," Jeff answers warily.

When his older sister wraps her arms around herself and makes kissing sounds, Jeff turns fire engine red.

I quit pummeling the meatloaf. "What's that supposed to mean?"

"Relax, Mom. All it means is that he's like every other boy in the sixth grade—He's got a crush on Miss Bliss." She scoots her chair closer to his. "Let me guess, she's taking the winner to a special lunch, off campus."

He slams his book shut. "Yeah, okay, what of it? That's just one of the perks."

She bats her eyes. "I'll say it is. Just make sure the maître d' seats you at a table that doesn't have a glass top. You wouldn't want to scare Miss Bliss off with a tent in your pants."

I almost drop the meatloaf on the way to the oven. "Okay, that's it, Mary! Up to your room. We'll call you down when dinner is ready."

Mary practically runs up the staircase. She's on the third step when I bark, "Leave your phone here, and you're forbidden to use email or IM accounts. No Facebook, Twitter, Instagram—nothing."

That stops her cold.

"I mean it. Drop the phone on the couch."

She's so angry that she starts to throw it, but reconsiders. Like all teens, her cell is her lifeline out of the Stones' desolate outpost in Siburbia.

Everyone is quiet as she stomps her way up the stairs, and over our heads on her way to her room.

Finally Trisha turns to Jeff and asks, "How do you make a tent in your pants?"

His face is flushed to the roots of his hair.

He's saved from answering by the creak of the back door as Aunt Phyllis enters. She practically stumbles under the weight of the box in her hands, plopping it down on the kitchen window seat. "Sounds like a party in here! What did I miss?"

Before Trisha can field that hot potato, Jack smacks his hand over her mouth. In unison, Jeff and I shout out, "Nothing!"

Her stare registers her obvious suspicion. "Okay, if you say so," she sniffs.

"Jeff was telling us he plans on running for class president—against Cheever."

Aunt Phyllis nods. "Good! Little bastard needs a comeuppance, and you're just the boy to give it to him."

"Will you help me with my platform, Aunt Phyllis?"

"Help you? Heck, consider me your campaign manager." She wipes her hands of dust from the box. "But first, some quid pro quo."

Jeff furrows his brow. "I know what that means. It's political speak for 'you scrub my back, and I'll scrub yours.'"

"Right! Only in this case, we won't take things so literal. Just seeing my wrinkly old hide would stunt your growth."

The last thing I need is for my son to hear sexual innuendos from my aunt. "What do you need, Aunt Phyllis?"

"A few helping hands. I got three more boxes in my car. They hold things that belong to you. I'd forgotten about them, until I went looking for my rollerblades"—seeing my eyes grow large, she adds, "Oh, don't worry! My skating days were over long ago. Let some other fool break a leg. But I sold them on Craig's List! Got my asking price, too—"

"Aunt Phyllis," I interrupt impatiently, "What were you saying about the boxes? How did you get a hold of them?"

"When you were off at college and your father died, I was left to clean out his house. Most of your dad's belong- ings were sold in garage sales, before the house itself was sold. But some of these items are keepers—the personal effects of your mother and your father."

Trisha raises her hand excitedly. "Mementoes!"

Aunt Phyllis nods. "You've got it, little one." She rewards my youngest with a kiss on the forehead. "In fact, Donna, I think there's even a few items you left behind."

I nod, but it's hard for me to say anything because I'm choked up at the thought of what those boxes may hold.

My mother died of cancer when I was only eleven. For the longest time she kept it a secret from my father and me while she prayed against all hope that her doctor would tell her it had gone into remission.

When it didn't, she still kept silent about her illness. To do otherwise would have shattered the image she had of herself as the ideal wife, perfect mother and consummate homemaker. The thought that she would be the cause of our devastating distress—that she could not be there to comfort us—was more than she could bear.

She had her wish. She fell into a coma before I knew the real cause of her "women's problems," as she called her fatigue and headaches.

She was right about one thing: we broke into a million little pieces.

Dad crawled into one bottle after another, and lost his liver for the love of Scotch.

I tried to replace her in his heart, but I couldn't. I found myself by learning to be a crack shot—and by losing my heart for the love of Carl.

I don't know what the boxes hold, but even now I'm not ready to open them. What good comes from looking back-ward? Things are never as we remember.

Just knowing the ghost of my mother can be summoned from dusty corners of a few old cardboard moving boxes has me tearing up. But instead of crying, I do what my mother would have done. I force my lips into a smile and exclaim, "Of course, Jack and Jeff will be glad to help you, Aunt Phyllis. The boxes can be stored in the garage, no problem."

Then I shoo Trisha toward the stairs, with the request that she call Mary to dinner.

I know how to hide my true self from others.

I am my mother's daughter, after all.

5

Whistle-Stopping

Back in the days when political candidates traveled by train, small towns were called whistle-stops. Politicians would use the stop to deliver a quick campaign speech, often from the back of the train, before heading to the next stop. Sometimes they'd stop in several towns in one day, giving the same speech, over and over again.

Today, to accomplish the same goal, they hop on the private jets of their biggest investors to get to the region in question. Then, with a cavalcade of gas-guzzling limos, hummers, or SUVs, they hit many events in neighborhoods that are demographically aligned with their policies.

In other words, places where they will be welcomed.

To walk into a place where you can face confrontation—and perhaps change a mind or two—is not a photo op; it is a crapshoot that few politicians are willing to take.

If you want a meal for your family that's a real crowd pleaser, this tried-and-true dish, originating from Spain, is perfect. It has been pleasing people all over the world for generations:

Picadillo (From Gayle Morell, Coconut Creek, Florida)

Ingredients

- 1 lb. of ground beef
- 1 tablespoon olive oil
- Cumin, to taste
- Adobo to taste
- Mexican chili powder to taste
- 1 large onion, chopped
- 4 garlic cloves, minced
- 2 (14-oz) cans diced tomatoes including juice (recommended: Original Rotel)
- 1/2 cup pimiento-stuffed green olives, coarsely chopped
- 2 cups rice
- 1 cup water

Directions

1. Make rice, by the directions.
2. Add olive oil to a pan and when it gets hot, add the onion and garlic.
3. When the onion is translucent, add the ground beef.
4. Add cumin, Adobo, and Mexican chili powder.

5. Cook until the meat is no longer pink. Drain any excess fat.
6. Add tomatoes and olives and allow to sit on low to medium heat until most of the liquid has been absorbed, but some remains to keep the meat moist.
7. Serve over rice.

THE SIGNS ALL OVER UCLA's AUDITORIUM READ: NO MORE MIDDLE EAST OCCUPATION!

Senator Franklin Percy is standing close enough to Jack that, through my ear bud, I can hear him murmur, "Great! Love that these kids are thinkers! Now, if they'll come to the polls, I'll give them what they want. The US has been in too many needless wars."

"Well, what do you know?" Abu's whisper also comes in loud and clear.

I'm surprised, too. Considering the senator's background, the last thing you'd expect is that he's more dove than hawk. Instead of supporting interminable wars in tribal countries that take too many lives and scar our soldiers for a lifetime, he rails against them. "If we truly want to protect America, start here, at home. Do it from our shores," he reasons.

His demand is met with a cacophony of applause.

Throughout the various events in Senator Franklin Percy's California whistle-stop campaign, the candidate never loses the twinkle in his piercing blue eyes, let alone his tight smile or his vise-like grip. His wave is more like a military salute, as are his close-cropped white hair and squared shoulders beneath shoulder-padded suit jackets.

From the senator's body language, I can tell he has taken to Jack, whose cover puts him front and center throughout the day. Granted, Jack is incognito: his hair is grayed, he wears a mustache, and glasses with video feedback to Arnie and Emma, who are manning a van with the insignia "KKKL-TV" with credentials that identify them as cameraman and producer, respectively.

The missus—Addie Franks Percy—is a thin, wan woman whose smile shifts between faint (if she's pleased) and benign (if she isn't). The senator's staff basically ignores her. The one aide who accompanies her only nudges her into the spotlight when the need calls for it.

My ID calls me out as the station's roving reporter, Brenda Stark. I've been equipped with a red wig, blue contact lenses, and the typical bland jacket-over-sheath ensemble that is considered just fashionable enough for couch potatoes to find me sexy, but not so hot haute couture that I stand out in the press corps, let alone the bevy of fawning acolytes, the hordes of protestors shouting against his mortgage lending bills, or the curious-but-undecideds.

Thus far, though, the mission has been uneventful. Granted, there were more protesters at the port of Long Beach than the VA hospital, but in both locations, they were kept at a distance, thanks to some sleight of hand by his savvy advance team.

The UCLA students have turned out to be a rowdier bunch than the Percy campaign anticipated. Percy's core message—to rebuild the US economy by providing the American people high-paying technology job opportunities in both the public and private sectors—should be just what they want to hear. Apparently no one presumed that students paying for a fairly high tuition in a sluggish economy would turn up their nose at this message.

"Greed is not good," is chanted in response to the senator's contention that protecting our financial institutions, at all costs is good for "your parents' investments in their homes, and in your education."

"When my parents lost their jobs, they lost their home, too," one yells from the back of the auditorium.

"Our tuition costs are sky high," yells another. "We pay more, and classes are cut because professors are being laid off. It's time our country put its money where its mouth is— make education free for all!"

Gracious condescension is the last thing a politician will find in a room filled with students who grew up honing their critical thinking skills. And yet, Senator Percy takes it all in stride.

"You're absolutely right," Percy agrees. "The Pentagon's seven-trillion-dollar budget is out of control. It's a black hole! Past presidents have found it impossible to audit. And yet, with the money we would save there, we'd have exactly that—the best educational system in the country. How badly do you want it? Only you can make change happen. You'll have to go to the polls to create the change you want."

"Awesome," murmurs the reporter to my right: some guy named Chuck Kessler who writes a blog called Truth Be Known. He points his iPhone in the direction of the protestor in order to capture the kid's angst up-close and personal, and jostles Arnie to do the same.

"What's wrong with you guys?" He chides us. "Even in the Yahooville you hail from, this should lead the seven o'clock news."

Arnie nods vigorously, then swings into action, pointing the camera and zooming in. I think he's forgotten the real reason we're here. At the very least, I hope he's scanning the crowd for anyone who may look suspicious.

His eyes roll over me. "Hey, Eye Candy! Make like a reporter and feed your camera man some color."

I'm about to tell him to make like a guy with two eyes and get the hell out of my face before he loses one of them to my fist when I notice a man, inching his way toward the stage. He's older than the average student, approximately thirty years of age. Of course, in this day and age of impacted classes, part-time students with chokehold loans and ongoing rounds of teacher layoffs, maybe it's taken him a decade to get his undergrad degree.

The man is tall, with olive skin and high cheekbones on a round face. His eyes are a startling blue. He wears a loose-fitting jacket over a button-down shirt and sweater vest. He waits patiently in the line in front of the microphone for those who want to ask the candidate a question.

Thus far, Percy has done a great job spinning his record, changing any question to something he'd prefer to answer, or staring down a heckler. Finally, it's the man's turn at the mike. He purses his lips and flexes his hands nervously. Yes, he's nervous. But why?

"Something's not right with him," I murmur into my mic to my mission team.

"Tracking," Abu answers, to indicate that he's within reach of the man, should he turn out to be the shooter.

Emma, who must have taken a facial recognition scan for assessment, responds "No criminal record. He's not on a watch list, either."

This has me breathing easier. On the other hand, a professional assassin might be hiding in plain sight, but wouldn't be standing in line to take a pot shot at his target. Still, you never know. "Do a cross-reference with the student and staff ID files," I suggest.

Finally the man reaches the microphone. Despite Percy's genial welcome and a brisk prod to speak up, the man sighs and stares down at his feet.

The crowd is getting uncomfortable, and I am, too.

Slowly, he reaches under his jacket and pulls something out—

At the same time Jack steps in front of Senator Percy, Abu comes at the man from one side, and I come at him from the other—

But he's not holding a gun.

It is a black and white photo: worn and frayed, obviously taken a couple of decades ago. He holds it up for the senator to see, then holds it up for the crowd. It shows a woman. She holds an infant in her arms, but she is frowning and tearful.

The man declares, "This is Carmen Diego de la Gregorio, a woman you raped thirty years ago, while you and the others under your command burned down my village in Panama during the United States' inglorious invasion of my country—the so-called 'Operation Just Cause.'" He pauses for a moment: "Senator Percy, I am the baby she holds in her arms. I am your son."

The room is shocked into silence, as is the senator.

But yes, the resemblance is there—in the broad shoulders, and the square-cut jaw.

In those startling blue eyes.

"I am the result of my mother's shame—and yours," the man continues. "Her shame over her rape caused her to kill herself, not soon after this picture was taken. I was put in an orphanage, where I … I too was subjected to atrocities. On the other hand, you came home a war hero." The man's bright blue eyes glimmer with tears yet to be shed. "Instead, you are a war criminal. You do not deserve to be the president of the United States."

Chuck nudges Arnie again. "Man, there's your money shot! Why isn't your camera rolling?"

Even if ours isn't, every other news camera is capturing Percy's shock and shame—not to mention all the cell phones in the room.

Percy doesn't deny the accusation. Nor does he signal the always-present but innocuous Acme security detail that has travelled with him here to Los Angeles.

Instead, he turns to his wife.

Tears are rolling down her cheeks, toward that enigmatic

grimace. "We have a child after all," she murmurs. "If he's willing to forgive you."

Percy holds out his hand to her. She hesitates, but takes it.

Together, they walk toward his son.

"WILL HE BE TRIED UNDER THE WAR CRIMES ACT?" I ASK JACK as we head home.

The implosion of Senator Franklin Percy's campaign has already spread like kudzu, strangling the twenty-four hour news cycle with innuendo, supposition and pundit pontification.

"It depends on several things. First, a DNA test must prove conclusively that the man is indeed Percy's son. And considering that the supposed rape took place over thirty years ago, does it fall under the War Crimes Act, which didn't exist until 1996? Such crimes are defined by the International Criminal Court, but our country doesn't accept its jurisdiction over our Armed Services."

"But Percy is retired military," I point out.

"Which throws another wrench in how it will be prosecuted, if at all," he reasons. "Another question to be answered is whether the Geneva Conventions put a statute of limitations on rape. And because the man's mother died at her own hand, Percy can't be tried for her murder, but certainly any emotional turmoil she had over the rape and pregnancy can be laid at his feet."

I check my iPhone for any news updates. "CNN just confirmed that Percy has agreed to a DNA test."

"I thought he might. Interestingly enough, he's not as upset as one might suspect over this."

"I thought it odd, too, until I heard Addie call the man 'our child.' She wanted him to come home with them."

"That won't mitigate Percy's actions." Jack pulls into our driveway and turns off the car. "Of all Percy's accomplishments, the one that eluded him was fatherhood. I know firsthand why both he and Addie are willing to accept the truth, no matter the consequences." He takes his right hand off the wheel in order to place it over mine. "The role I play in your children's lives filled a big hole in my life. I'll always appreciate your decision to share them with me."

"You will always be their father, Jack."

"Thanks, Donna. I know you mean that from the bottom of your heart. But won't a time come when we have to tell them the truth?"

"No." I turn away from him. "Carl is gone. We've made sure of that."

He turns my face toward him. "There are other ways in which the children may find out. Last night, all the time I'm sitting there with Trisha, working on her memento project, I'm thinking to myself, 'When will she notice that I'm not in any of her pictures?' If not Trisha, then maybe Jeff will wonder about it. And let's not forget that Mary was eight when Carl disappeared. Her memories of him may be fuzzy, but someday something may trigger one that doesn't reconcile with her life as she knows it."

"We've had that test already, Jack! Mary met Carl, and talked to him. She described him as 'creepy.'"

"Maybe 'creepy' was her way of describing a deep-seated memory of him." He shrugs. "You and I both know that all it takes is a DNA test to shatter the myth we're living. Percy is proof of that. Donna, I'm just suggesting that we consider why, how and when we'd break the news to the children."

"Jack, your presence in their lives, every day, is why you're their father, not some chromosome test. So are the many little acts of love you do on their behalves." I tighten my hand in his. "We better get inside. Jeff just texted me that he wants me to make six dozen of my killer peanut butter chocolate chip cookies to hand out tomorrow before the election."

He nods. "Trisha and I are finishing her project tonight."

I don't want to hurt him anymore, but I have to ask. "Are you anywhere on her board?"

That puts a smile on his face. "She saved the wrapper from the very first ice cream cone I bought her. I couldn't believe it. When I asked her why, she said, 'Because I'd never seen Mommy so happy than that day.'"

I laugh. "What a perceptive young lady. If you want to keep that smile on my face, why don't you kiss me now?"

He does.

She's right, nothing makes me happier.

6

Rubber Chicken Circuit

The endless series of public dinners and luncheons politicians must attend to raise funds and make speeches is called "the rubber chicken circuit," due to the fact that the main course is usually the domesticated fowl in question, and that more than likely the hotel which serves it, cooked it hours earlier, and then reheated it, giving it a rubbery texture.

"Eating crow" is another political culinary term of note, and sometimes used in tandem with this one—especially in instances when a microphone is left on while the candidate is enjoying a candid moment with a trusted confidante. Saying something like, "Do you think they believed that bunch of hooey?" or exclaiming, "How 'bout them ta-tas on that gal in the front row..." will certainly have any politician wishing he'd kept his yap shut, as opposed to putting his foot in it.

Juiciest Roast Chicken Ever (From Ally Rusu, Sausalito, California)

Ingredients

- Large whole Chicken
- ½ Cup of Olive Oil
- 1 Cup Vodka
- Salt
- Pepper
- Garlic Powder
- 1/3 Onion

Directions

1. Preheat Oven to 350 degrees.
2. Clean the chicken of all inside bags, and wash well.
3. Slice the onion, in ringlets. Set aside.
4. Put the chicken in a roasting pan and season generously, inside and out, with salt, pepper, and garlic powder.
5. Brush olive oil on the inside of the bird's cavity, then outside as well.
6. Add the vodka and onions to the cavity.
7. Bake, uncovered, for 1 hour and 15 minutes, in the preheated oven.
8. Remove from heat, and baste with drippings.
9. Cover with aluminum foil, and allow to rest about

30 minutes before serving.

"WISH ME LUCK," JEFF SAYS, AS HE HOPS OUT OF MY CAR. HE'S recruited Morton to help him carry and distribute his campaign paraphernalia: posters that say, "Equal Rights for All! Vote Jeff for Class President" as well as buttons, and of course my cookies.

At least, those that Morton hasn't already eaten.

"Break a leg!" Trisha yells after him.

"Next stop, Babs' house," I declare.

Mary and Wendy, who have been whispering furiously in the van's back seat, freeze. "Um … no need, Mom. She's gotten another ride to school."

"With whom?" If that were the case, Babs' mother, Janine, would have called me. We carpool because Babs' parents are going through a bitter divorce. Janine gets up early for her shift at our local hospital.

"Just … someone at school." Guilt is written all over Mary's face.

The boy—what was his name again? Oh yeah, Blake McAllister.

I stop the car. "Who is it, Mary?"

The girls exchange glances.

"Mom, don't be mad, but …"

I hold my breath.

"She's biking in."

"But … why?"

"Because I told her I thought it would be best if we weren't seen together." Mary shifts uncomfortably in her seat. "Mom, nobody likes her at school."

Trisha frowns. "But *you* like her—don't you?"

Mary shrugs. "I used to. But sometimes people change."

"Just last week, the three of you were the best of friends," I point out. "It's been that way since the three of you started kindergarten together. Tell me, Mary, who has changed, you, or Babs? And if so, how? Why?"

Wendy and Mary exchange glances. Finally Wendy says, "Erin doesn't like her. She knows Blake thinks she's cute. If we hang with Babs, we'll be pegged as losers, too. And we're not!"

"Mom, you don't know what they're saying about Babs! They say that she's putting out. They write mean things about her on Facebook. They write messages to all the people she's friended there, and ask if they're losers, too. It's not our fault that Babs made an enemy of the most popular girl in school."

"No, not at all. But it's also not Babs' fault that she's pretty, and that some boy thinks so, too. And it will be your fault if you desert your friend now, when she needs you more than ever. How would you feel if you were the one being deserted?"

In unison, the girls blanch at this thought.

"I … I hadn't thought of it that way," Mary admits. "We'll work it out."

I smile at her through the rearview mirror. "I know you'll do the right thing."

If only she'd smile back.

Instead, she opens her history book and pretends to read.

"It's always such a joy to visit the great state of California," purrs Governor Rebecca Davis to her *Good Afternoon LA!* host. "The folks here are so warm and friendly!" She points to the bouquet of flowers in her lap. "A little girl gave me this—your California poppies, are they not? Such a bright spot of color! Too bad she's not old enough to vote!"

This Southerner, whose honeyed homilies are delivered with icy smiles, is the next candidate entrusted to our care.

The interview is being taped in her swanky suite, high in the Casa del Mar, a hotel overlooking Santa Monica Beach along its renowned boardwalk. The brilliant blue sky and azure ocean make a wonderful backdrop for the photo op. The protestors who hate Governor Davis must realize this, too, because they stand below the balcony, chanting slogans that mock her policies against the things that affect their lives (a livable minimum wage), liberties (pro-choice), and pursuits of happiness (gay marriage).

We've been with her since early this morning. The first stop was a breakfast with a group of ministers from various conservative congregations, all of whom revel in the knowledge that they have a candidate who will advance their agenda. The same can be said for her lunch with California's largest gun rights advocate group, and tonight's dinner with the petrochem lobby.

This is one lady who enjoys preaching to the choir. But what waits for her outside the comfy confines of her hotel is anything but that.

The few steps that took her from one hotel lobby to her motorcade to her next stop at her hotel were a daunting gauntlet. Arnie walked ahead, while Jack and Dominic flanked her on either side, Abu was close on her tail, and her prim and mousy press secretary, Susannah Jenner, was, as always, by her side.

Like little chicks, the rest of her advance team fanned out after them: a pollster, her scheduler, her California precinct organizers, and various and sundry volunteers.

The protesters who screamed and shouted at her are just as alarmed about her as she is about them. It freaks them out that she consistently votes down any attempt at gun control legislation, despite a recent mass shooting at a school in her state. And although the US government has ruled that gay spouses of National Guard members will be provided the same federal marriage benefits as heterosexual spouses, hers was one of the few states that pulled benefits from all spouses rather than comply.

Upon her return, she held her head high as she glided through the hotel's sliding doors like a beauty queen who has already been bequeathed her coveted tiara. Her disdain for those who don't agree with her position is just a wee less condescending than those whose votes are a slam-dunk, including a woman holding up a little girl, who practically forced the governor to take the bouquet of poppies in her hand.

If a camera hadn't been pointed in her direction, I don't think she would have bothered. She's the perfect example of *be careful what you wish for*.

Now that the interview is in full swing, I'm set up in the room next to the interview suite, which keeps me close at hand. Arnie has me tapped into the hotel security cam, so that we can watch from my television monitor. We can also pick up the production crew's camera feed, so that I have eyes and ears on the interview, too.

Jack's orders are to stay with the candidate at all times. Dominic and Abu are covering the door.

The interview is going smoothly, for the most part. The reporter is lobbing softballs, and the governor is hitting them out of the park: about her hardscrabble childhood, her popularity as a cheerleader, and her beauty pageant wins that gave her the scholarship to law school, where she met her husband, a burly college linebacker named Jim Bob.

"I ended up with a JD, and an MRS," she exclaims slyly.

With her gumption and gift for gab, politics was a natural. She claims to have "a Tupperware approach" to campaigning: "Make every event a party, and make that sale," she pronounces proudly.

"But you don't invite everyone to your 'party,'" the reporter counters.

"Even at a party, there are rules of decorum. If you don't play by the rules, you don't get invited back." Her tone may be all moonlight and magnolias, but her smile is brittle as black ice.

Suddenly, the sounds below us get my attention. The protesters are chanting, "Go! Go! Go!"

Who's going where?

I run out to my balcony to see what's up.

Some guy is climbing from one balcony to another. He has just pulled himself onto the one connected to the governor's suite and is about to open the door when I leap onto it myself.

He is on an adrenaline rush that comes with knowing you're a hero to your cause. No way is he going to let me stand in the way of that. He rushes me, only to get kicked in the gut. As he falls over the ledge, he grapples for my hand—

But he's too heavy for me. I lose my balance. We're both about to go over the balcony when someone grabs me by my legs—

Jack.

The guy can no longer hold on. He falls into the hotel's pool.

On the other hand, I'm pulled back over the rail, by Jack. He huddles over me, whispering, "You're okay … you're okay …."

Yes, because he's here to protect me.

To love me.

But Ryan is yelling through our ear buds, warning Jack not to leave the governor unprotected.

"You can't be here with me," I mumble into his chest. "Go to her."

But he doesn't. "You're my first priority, forever."

"Ditto," I mutter.

He nods. Then he gets up and runs after the candidate and her posse, who are in full retreat.

Yes, there will be hell to pay.

Governor Davis' anger flows out of her in syrupy waves. Everyone within spitting distance gets caught in the sour sorghum of her fear, but it's Jack who gets the brunt of it. "What the hell were you doing, covering that one, there?" She points to me. "Some bodyguards! Y'all are as useless as a teat on a boar hog."

Okay, yeah, whatever that means.

Apparently Jack speaks some Southernese because he retorts, "Governor, don't go off with your pistol half-cocked. Donna protected you from a protestor who came up the balcony, intent on interrupting your interview. Feel free to thank her for doing so."

"Thank you—I guess." She shrugs in my direction. "Well, you can't blame me for being hotter than a two-dollar pistol. I'm not used to my security team taking off into the sunset and leaving me exposed to all of California's fruits and nuts."

I know better than to speak up, seeing that my own collo-quialisms aren't as colorful, but more graphic in nature. A single finger, pointed skyward, say.

"I'm only gonna chew this cabbage once, so pay atten-tion, y'all," she continues. "I don't like to be pushed or shoved or shouted at. So keep that scum out there as far away from me as possible." She shivers. "Or next time, I'll pull out my Smith & Wesson, and take down each of those bellyachers myself."

"Becca, get control of yourself," Susannah murmurs.

"Damn it, Susannah! You and I both know that back home they'd be applauding me for taking on that riffraff down there—not to mention the NRA, which would love to see me all brassy and sassy and taking no prisoners." She waves us away. "Hell, their donations are practically bankrolling this campaign, anyway. I say we give 'em something they'll be proud of."

Seeing Jack's frown, she adds, "Look, just because half the country is on the dole doesn't mean I have to kiss their deadbeat asses. Maybe if we offer the great state of California to the Chinese as a present, they'll finally leave us alone. All they want is Silicon Valley anyway."

Jack forces his wince into a smile. "Governor, do you really wish to hand over the twelfth largest economy in the world, and thirteen percent of the US gross domestic product, to another super power?"

His admonishment has her turning the same soft pink shade as her crepe wool suit. "How dare you speak to me like that! Who do you think you are!" She's so angry that she's shaking. "My life is a living hell, mister! Do you think I like having your California wing nuts climbing through my window? Do you know what it's like to have people always wanting something from you? They think you walk on water, that you can solve all their problems. And those are just the little people, not the ones who toss you a few sawbucks, then expect you to prostitute yourself for them." Her words come out in fits and sobs. "I have to smile on cue, and talk on cue, and pretend to like someone on cue. I also have to pretend to be … to be …what I'm not."

She's just about to lay into him again, when two members of her advance team run into the room. "Governor, are you still mic'd?" Her pollster asks.

Exasperated, Rebecca shakes her head, and waves them away.

Her scheduler looks confused. "But—but every word you're saying is live, now—on every network!"

"It can't be. The news team is gone, and they took the sound package with them," Arnie explains.

"This room must be bugged," I answer.

Jack puts a finger to his lips to warn the governor and her staff to be quiet, then he flicks on the television.

Yes, there it is, live on one of the cable news networks, under the headline, "Stupid Politician Tricks." A still shot of Governor Davis, a dimpled smile on her face, is being shown. The delayed recording plays on until it catches up to the bump and clatter of Arnie, Dominic, Abu, Jack and me as we climb the walls, literally, pulling apart light fixtures and vents, and flipping over cushions and furniture.

When Jack picks up the bouquet of poppies and shakes it, we see it:

The sound bug.

He hands it to Arnie, who will attempt to trace its source.

"I'm ruined! My political career is over!" Rebecca Davis

gasps for air as she drops onto the couch and buries her face in her hands.

Susannah crouches beside her to pat her arm and hug her shoulder.

To shush her, and kiss her cheek.

This small act of kindness transforms her boss.

Her back turns to steel, and once again her face is a Kabuki mask of imperiousness, and it is turned our way. "Leave please, everyone."

Everyone but Susannah heads out the door.

"Maybe now she'll finally come out of the closet," the pollster mutters to the scheduler.

The other woman clicks her tongue. "Poor Jim Bob."

The pollster cocks her head. "What are you talking about? He's known all along."

"Oh, I wasn't talking about that, hon," the scheduler assures her. "He was looking forward to sleeping in Lincoln's bedroom."

The pollster smirks. "Yeah, and so was his mistress."

Ah, politics as usual.

7

Political Cooler

Someone who has a history of bad luck while managing a campaign is known as a political cooler.

You don't necessarily have to be in politics to cool a great running streak for someone else. For example, every time you put your foot in your mouth in front of your husband's boss, more than likely you've cooled his chance of getting a raise.

Should you ruin enough opportunities for him, a lot of cheap meals, like pasta, may be in your future. Here's a wonderful and cost effective pasta dinner—and you can serve it cool, too:

Parslied Fettuccini (From Linda Quick, Waverly New York)

Ingredients

- 1 Pound of Fettuccini
- 1 large Bunch of fresh Parsley

- 1/2 Cup ground Pine Nuts or Walnuts
- 1 Can of Pitted Black Olives (drained)
- 1 block of crumbled feta cheese (about 6 - 8 ounces)
- Lemon juice
- Garlic
- Olive oil

Directions

1. While boiling pasta, sauté several cloves of garlic in a small amount of olive oil (approx.).
2. Wash and chop the parsley, adding to the garlic (once it's cooked).
3. Add the ground nuts and lemon juice (1/8 - 1/4 cup).
4. Mix with the olives and feta then toss over pasta.

"WELL, WELL, WELL, MR. AND MRS. STONE! FIRST A Democratic frontrunner implodes on your watch, followed by the GOP's little darling." Ryan's attempt at sarcasm at my expense has everyone on my Acme team wincing. "I've got both parties wondering if they've hired a team of political coolers."

"The fact that Senator Percy's past came back to haunt him certainly wasn't our faults," I point out.

"But letting a protester get that close to the governor—

while she was filming an interview, no less—was certainly a black eye." Ryan shrugs.

"So sorry! I was pre-occupied at the time—hanging off a balcony." I'm being a smart ass, and he knows it.

"Not to mention allowing her conversation to be bugged." He loves to rub salt in the wound.

"In all fairness, Ryan, Arnie swept the room twice before the interview," Jack reminds him. "If the governor hadn't insisted on using the flowers as a prop, it would have never happened."

Ryan sighs. "This is like Watergate all over again."

"Speaking of which, have any of the other campaigns 'fessed up to it?" I ask.

"The leak originated with a blog called 'Truth Be Known', run by someone called Chuck Kessler. The other political bloggers call him, 'Chuck the Muckraker.'"

"Catchy," Emma sniffs.

The name rings a bell. "Hey, Arnie and I met him! He was at Percy's UCLA talk."

Ryan lets that sink in. "That puts him at the scene of the crime twice. Arnie, see if you can hack his computer and find out how he got his hands on that audio feed. He may also be the key to the rumors of the assassination attempts." He shakes his head. "That leaves each party with just one frontrunner—and the Democratic candidate, Senator Randolph Oliver Jennings, will be in town early tomorrow, in fact."

"His whole campaign is based on funding renewable energy businesses!" Emma sounds awed at the prospect.

"Yes, that's right. On his itinerary are tours of a solar field, an offshore wind turbine project, and a farm that is a model for a national sustainable farming program." He frowns. "Of course, he's got his detractors."

"Let me guess: Big Agra," Emma mutters.

"Frankly, his largest opposition comes from armament manufacturers. Whereas he sits on the Senate's Energy and Water Development committee, they grind their teeth because he is also a senior member of the Senate committees for Homeland Security, and Defense, where he advocates for arms control, especially when it comes to drones, anti-cluster munitions, and landmines."

"I presume the NRA also sees him as a foe," Dominic says.

Ryan nods. "That goes without saying. Because he's made himself a target on many fronts, safeguarding him won't be easy. But unfortunately, except for an evening fundraiser, all of his photo ops are in the great outdoors, so you'll have your work cut out for you. His plane arrives tomorrow morning at eight, at John Wayne." He turns to Arnie. "Your first priority is Chuck the Muckraker, so sit this one out. Emma can monitor surveillance."

In unison, Arnie and Emma give Ryan a thumbs-up— then again in unison, they blush when they realize this.

Ah, young love.

Ryan's last words of caution give us pause as we make our way out the door: "We can't afford another black eye, people, so let's keep this candidate in play."

I get to Trisha's school earlier than anticipated, so I park and walk into the lobby to wait for her release. School has only been in session a few days, but with all of our mission assignments, it seems as if it's been a million years since that very first day of school.

The first thing that greets me in the reception area is a scaled-down 3-D cardboard model of a major university. I'm trying to figure out where I've seen it before. Is it Oxford, or Cambridge? And why is it here? Is it an older student's project? If so, the child deserves an A plus plus.

I've just stooped to look at the tiny cardboard people in the building's windows when I hear Lee Chiffray's voice, next to my ear: "Beautiful isn't it?"

My instinct is to straighten up, but I know if I do, we'll bump right into each other. Instead, I turn my head slightly, only to find myself looking into his deep blue eyes.

He's studying me. Why?

"It's incredible. Is it a student project?"

That brings a hearty laugh from him. "I hope not, considering I ponied up a pretty penny for it. It's a model from the architectural plans for Hilldale Elementary, which was designed by one of the top architectural firms in the country."

"What? Why, for goodness sake?"

He shrugs. "As you can see, the members of the school's redevelopment committee have been busy little bees. Over the past few days they've been polling—I guess a better word for it would be strong-arming—all the parents into submitting a wish list for a world-class school."

I let loose with a low whistle. "When I walked in here, I thought I was looking at a model for Oxford University."

He chuckles. "You're close. Frankly, it's a model of Hogwarts."

I take a closer look. "Oh my god, you're right! The students are even wearing silks! The only things missing are the witch's caps and the owls!"

Now we're both laughing—so loudly in fact, that the librarian sticks her head out the door and shushes us.

Lee waves at her, then steers me out of the lobby, into the playground. We're too large for the swings, so he motions me to sit on the slide.

I forget I'm in shorts. When the backs of my thighs hit the slide's hot tin, I yelp and leap back up.

"Sorry, I didn't think ..." His ears turn red. He is truly embarrassed by the incident.

Charming.

Yes, I want to like him, to be his friend.

At the same time, I have so many questions to ask him.

No, really, there is only one question that matters:

Is he a member of the Quorum?

If I were to ask him—right now just out of the blue— would he tell me?

Of course not. Because I am the enemy.

The best way to judge him is by actions, not his words.

"So, what's your opinion on all this?" he asks.

If only you knew.

Finally I say, "I think it's scary. A fancy building isn't what makes an education great. It's about the people who run the programs, and giving them the necessary resources to do so."

He lets that sink in.

Yes, I would like to know what he thinks, too. But do I trust him to tell me the truth, or to give me only what he thinks I want to hear?

Instead of asking, I change the subject yet again. "I don't know what these parents are thinking. Seriously, who'd foot the bill on a massive project like this?"

"They haven't thought it through yet. You see, the parents here are caught up in the dream, in the glory of it all." He shakes his head. "This is a reflection of their egos. But when push comes to shove—when it's time to pay the piper, reality will set in." He shrugs. "And we'll be back where we started."

"So, you're saying this was an exercise in futility?"

"No, not at all. My offer still stands, and always will." He leans in, as if telling me a secret: "In the end, Donna, the only thing that matters is that you get what you want. Unfortunately, we don't all want the same things."

I'm tempted to ask him what exactly he wants—from me, but the next thing I know my daughter is jumping into my arms.

Now is not the time or the place to ask.

It will come soon enough.

JEFF'S LONG FACE TELLS ME ALL I NEED TO KNOW:

He lost the election.

He hops in, slams the car door, and slumps below the window. "I just don't understand what happened! All the exit polls—"

I turn to face him. "Your class conducted exit polls?"

He looks at me as if I landed just from Mars. "Yes, of course! It's an election, Mom. People wanted to gauge the accuracy of the pre-election polls and pundits' predictions."

"Well, at least you don't have to wait four more years to run again."

"In fact, I might, if Cheever has his way. He's pulling a Tajikistan—you know, extending the election cycle—only by three years, not forever. He claims it will have a stabilizing effect on the administration's policies, but he knows it's because we'll be in high school after that."

"What policies? I'd imagine the biggest issues you face in the sixth grade are whether to lobby for bigger lockers or more recess."

He rolls his eyes. "Back in your day, maybe, but this is the Twenty-first Century. We've got real issues. There are subcommittees on everything from classroom etiquette, to dress code, bus rules, homework policy, conflict resolution, social events—you get the idea."

No, not really. But I'm not willing to admit how out of touch I am with his world.

I guess he's smart enough to do his own laundry now.

For that matter, the rest of the family's too.

And his math skills are decent. Should I test him on the household QuickBooks budget sheets?

Suddenly my world has opened up immensely.

And since I'm into quid pro quo, I'll go ahead and ask: "Hey, Jeff, what are the chances that Cheever tampered with the votes?"

He thinks for a moment, then nods. "Votes are tabulated electronically. A code is needed to access it. We've still got the paper ballots as a check system."

"Great. I'm sure Arnie would be glad to run an audit, if you ask him."

Jeff frowns. "Do you think he still holds a grudge because I almost stole Emma from him?"

I hope my laughing fit sounds like a very bad cough. When I recover, I murmur, "I'd be willing to bet he's gotten over it by now."

"Okay then, sure. Let's put him to work."

The kid is already sounding presidential.

Senator Randolph Oliver Jennings comes with no entourage. He insists on being called Randy, and wears jeans and a blue work shirt, like the men who work the fields that surround us here in California's Central Valley. Both are worn and frayed, not at all like the crisp new duds that other politicians don for their photo ops. His hands are not soft and pliable, but chapped and tanned, attesting to his love of the great outdoors, and his humble beginnings as a farmer.

He asks the right questions—about weather patterns and crop conditions; about the equipment needs and loans and subsidies.

He isn't afraid to answer the ones thrown back at him. His answers are forthright and he refuses to dodge the hard ones. He will admit, for example, that it may take years, if not decades for alternative fuel technology to be commercially viable.

"Harnessing it is the easy part," he explains. "Making it sustainable—that is, dropping it into a current energy delivery system, is the missing link. But it starts here, with you," he declares to the farmers who have gathered to hear him. "You are ground zero, because you have the land."

"If the government gave us the money we need to do it right, we could stay in business—and on our land," someone shouts back.

Randy chuckles. "Amen, brother. That's why I need your votes."

I stand with a battery of reporters. I am not at all surprised to see Chuck the Muckraker among them. He taps away furiously on his cell. I presume he's taking notes. We'll find out as soon as Emma can scan his cell phone.

The guy is tech-savvy enough to frustrate Arnie, who has yet to break Chuck's firewall, even with Ryan pacing in and out of his lair.

At Randy's behest, only Dominic stands beside him, ready to be a human shield if the situation calls for it. Like me, Abu and Jack cover the crowd. In this crowd, guns are as common as cowboy hats and boots. Yes, some are skeptical, but more are desperate to monetize their land, so they will set aside the smart-ass barbs and listen to what the man from Washington, DC has to say.

Every now and then, a phone will beep or buzz, or croon a favorite country tune. Quickly it is silenced, so that Randy can get on with what he has to say.

But right when he's trying to make a very important point, Chuck stops him in mid-sentence and asks, "Senator, when was the last time you heard from your son?"

"I … what?" He blinks, as if caught in a glaring light.

"I asked you about your son, Sam." Chuck holds up his iPhone, as if taping the conversation.

"He's studying abroad."

"Where, may I ask?"

"He's in India."

"Not even close." Chuck smiles smugly. "He's in Afghanistan, isn't he? Not with our armed forces, but fighting them with the Taliban, under the name of Ahmad Navid Ali."

The crowd murmurs its shock, some at the audacity of the reporter's questions, and others because they find it disturbing that Randy doesn't laugh incredulously at the accusation, let alone declare him a liar in no uncertain terms.

"Senator Jennings, is this your son?" Chuck holds up his phone so that those closest can see the screen. On it, a young, blond man in desert garb declares in clear, concise English, his wish that those brothers of Allah listening to this video will follow his instructions for martyrdom for the most right-eous cause of defeating the devils who now swarm

Afghanistan with their drones and planes and soldiers and guns. He demonstrates the best way to wrap explosives around your body, how to conceal them within your coat, how to avoid the telltale signs that you are doing so, and how to enter an army base. Better yet, choose a shopping mall or a library.

Finally, he closes by wishing them a speedy journey to Allah.

Randy stands there, frozen, like the Tin Man stuck in the field during a rainstorm.

What can he say when Chuck asks him how he has the audacity to sit on the Senate Intelligence Committee, let alone the one for Homeland Security?

The one thing Randy is not is audacious.

He walks away from the crowd that is now anxious and angry, without saying a word.

As we drive him back to the airport, the radio stays off.

The five-hour flight to DC gives him plenty of time to prepare his resignation speech.

Forget the sins of the father. The sins of the son are just as deadly, if the goal is character assassination.

8

Muckraker

A journalist who exposes the activities of politicians behaving badly is called a "muckraker." This term comes from John Bunyan's book, The Pilgrim's Progress, which had a character called the Man with the Muck Rake because he was so obsessed with the muck of worldly profit, he could never look up.

When looking down, you may hear a lot, but you miss a lot, too—especially in journalism, a profession where you need your eyes as well as your ears, to see things for yourself.

Today's journalists don't rely on either their eyes or their ears. They have the Internet. Why actually get your hands dirty digging for facts when you can just quote some source without determining if the information has been vetted?

Quick and Easy Quiche (From Toni Meehan, West Bend, Wisconsin)

Ingredients

- Box of Stove Top stuffing.
- Spinach, broccoli or some other vegetable and/or ham or some other meat
- 6 eggs
- 1 12-oz can of Evaporated Milk
- 4-6 Cups Cheese (Feta, Jarlsberg or Sharp Cheddar are some choices, depending on whether you want creamy texture and mild, or sharp flavor; Hard cheese should be shredded.)
- Salt and Pepper

Directions

1. Follow the directions on the box to make the stuffing, then split between 2 pie plates.
2. To each shell, add cheese; usually 2-3 cups.
3. Then add meat and/or veggie, if you like.
4. In separate bowl, mix 6 eggs with a 12 oz. can of evaporated milk; split between the two pies.
5. Salt and pepper to your taste.
6. Bake at 350 for about 45 minutes, until golden brown on top and knife in center comes out clean.

"THE CIA IS LIVID," RYAN SHOUTS AT ALL OF US.

"I take it they didn't know about Senator Jennings' son?" Jack asks.

"On the contrary, Sam Jennings is one of their undercover agents. He infiltrated the Taliban five years ago, under deep cover. Under an assumed name, he began attending a mosque in Detroit. He connected with one of their stateside recruiters, who viewed him as a perfect candidate for the next level of jihad—the disillusioned youth of America. Now, not only has this leak sabotaged his father's presidential candidacy and a stellar political career, it has also put Sam's life in danger."

"I have friendly eyes and ears within the Pakistani Inter-Services Intelligence. I'll initiate contact to find out if anything has happened to the young man," Dominic offers.

"Good idea. I hope we don't bring more bad news the senator's way." Ryan turns to me. "In the meantime, we need to find Chuck the Muckraker, and find out who's his Deep Throat. You said you've met him?"

"Yes, Chuck knows me as a fellow reporter, and Arnie as my camera man."

"Good. Get close, and use that to your advantage."

"Will do, boss," I assure him.

"Speaking of getting close, Jack mentioned that the Chiffrays have enrolled their daughter in Trisha's class."

"Yes, it's true." I feel a blush creeping up my neck.

"Well, that's a lucky break for us."

"Why is that?"

"The stuff Dominic has been getting from our cousins

across the pond certainly makes him a person of interest in regard to our Quorum investigation."

"You mean, the purchase of the Kensington townhome?"

"One and the same."

"Couldn't it have just been a coincidence?"

"Yes, it could have been—except for the fact that he's also the new leaseholder on the Quorum's villa in Cabo San Lucas, not to mention his firm also owns Fantasy Island, as you recall. You know what they say: where there's smoke, there's fire. That being said, if you get the opportunity to get close to Babette, take it."

"As of yet, she hasn't shown up at any school functions."

"That's odd. Jack mentioned the Chiffrays were heading up some sort of school fundraiser."

"They are—that is, Lee is heading up the endeavor."

Ryan's eyes light up. "Even better. I'm sure you can find some reason to get cozy."

I nod, and head out the door.

I don't need to chase after Lee. My guess is that the fundraiser is his excuse to be near me.

I just wish I knew why.

THE OFFICIAL OFFICE OF *TRUTH BE KNOWN* IS A DINGY COTTAGE on an alley in Venice. Because he knows me as Brenda Stark, girl reporter, I'm back in my red wig. This time I've added a push-up bra and stilettos, as an inducement for Chuck to open up.

It also helps that I've brought along a thimbleful of SP-117, a drug that loosens the tongue, but hazes the brain afterward. He'll never even remember I was there.

While Chuck is spilling his guts to me, Arnie will download the stroke history of Chuck's computer, then release a Remote Access Trojan so that we can follow his every move.

We've just pulled up in the KKKL-TV van when we notice someone is already on the front stoop.

Two someones, in fact. They are NSA agents. We know not because of any psychic abilities or my women's intuition, but because they yell it out before breaking down the front door of the cottage.

Just as they do, a big-breasted, bowlegged blond floozy in a tight white cocktail frock runs out the back. But when the strap comes loose on one of her pink and blue kitten heel shoes, she gets tripped up and falls on her face.

"That's our man," I say to Arnie. "Quick, pull up alongside of him."

Arnie tilts his head, puzzled. "Really? How can you tell?"

"No self-respecting woman wears white after Labor Day, let alone shoes that ugly. And besides, his wig is on backwards."

"Gotcha." We're there in a flash.

I bat my eyes at Chuck. "Nasty fall! Need a lift?"

When he recognizes me, he does a double-take. "Brenda? What are you doing here?"

"We're about to shoot a segment on the Venice Beach musclemen. You know, show the yahoos that there are ways to pump up other than farm chores." I lower my sunglasses to take in the vision before me. "You know, I almost didn't recognize you at first. Who knew Chuck the Muckraker had such gorgeous gams!"

"Shhhh, not so loud! I'm incognito!" He puts his finger to his lips as he glances sideways down the block. "Those men are Federal agents! They think I tapped into the NSA's database, and then leaked the intel from it on my website. Of course, even if I did, I'd be protected by my First Amendment rights."

"Good to know. Why don't we call them over and remind them?"

Hearing that, he turns as white as his dress.

"Listen, you Snowden wannabe, you better jump in before they come over and ask you for a date. You're much too pretty for the boys of Gitmo."

He gets it. He tosses his computer bag into the back seat, then climbs in after it. The threshold on the van's door is high enough that he has to hike up his frock before hopping in, giving me more than an eyeful of his tighty-whities.

Arnie must be blinded by the sight because he steps on the gas, but stops short before hitting the car in front of us.

The syringe with the SP-117 flies out the window.

"Oops," Arnie mutters.

Time to punt. Forcing a smile, I turn to Chuck. "If you're going to make a habit of playing dress-up, I've got to introduce you to Spanx. And this, too. Trust me, it'll bring out the roses in your cheeks." I pull out a lip wand labeled *Cherry Noir*. Smiling, I apply a little gloss on his lips. "So that it spreads evenly, do this." I smack my lips then lick them.

It's a custom brand carried only by Acme honeypots. The smack does the job of spreading the color. The lick does the trick of drugging him so that he passes out.

As Arnie roars off down the street, he asks, "Where should we take him?"

Good question. It's not as if we can waltz him into Acme's offices. And I've got the guest-who-won't-leave staying in the bonus room over my garage, so that's out, too.

Suddenly I have a brilliant idea. I dial Dominic. "Meet me at your new place. You're about to host your very first guest."

Dead silence, then the sputtering starts. "My dear, are you mad? Chateau Fleming is far from ready to receive visitors! There is still much finish work to do. The *rake facia* on the cornices is off by a quarter of an inch, not to mention the entry foyer's hardwood floor has yet to be stenciled with my family seal—"

"Dominic, it ain't the Queen who's dropping by. I'm talking … well, torture, if it comes to that."

"Ah, I see." He sighs. "Well, at least *that* room is complete."

I'm not surprised. Dominic has a very active social life.

When we get through with Chuck, he's going to wish he'd gone with the Feds.

IN TRUTH, DOMINIC'S TORTURE ROOM IS A PLEASURE GROTTO FOR

the senses, with spa, steam room, workout suite, indoor pool, yoga room and massage alcove.

But when one is blindfolded, even a six-person indoor Jacuzzi spa with forty-four PowerPro luxury jets letting loose with a force equivalent to Niagara Falls can seem as ominous as a waterboarding bucket.

When it comes to making this extraordinary chamber sound like the seventh circle of Hell, Dominic is a pro. I guess it has something to do with spending twelve years in an English all-boy's private prep school.

With all the pomposity of Voldemort, he explains to the prisoner the process in which we will extract the information we need. First, he will be stripped down (yes, the tighty-whities will have to go) and forced to stand for a long time in extreme heat (the sauna room) while being subjected to extreme duress (Metallica, played over a Bose Acoustic Wave stereo system) in contorted positions. (One of Dominic's new lady friends is a Bikram yoga instructor who doubles as a dominatrix. Just a wild guess, but I presume the mantra chanted most often by her disciples is "I feel the pain!")

If he still doesn't break, he is told he will be shackled and stretched until his muscles are forever useless (thank you, Bowflex Revolution Home Gym). "Then there is the water-boarding." As a special effect, Dominic splashes his hand in the Jacuzzi's roiling tub, and the scent of rose petals wafts through the air.

I wish he hadn't done that, since it sort of defeats the purpose of scaring him in the first place.

As it turns out, Chuck is a bigger weenie than I would

have imagined. He whimpers from the moment he is tossed into the sauna. Before a half-hour is out, he breaks. "I don't know where the information comes from, I swear!" He screams over Metallica's *Whiskey in the Jar*. "It's always anonymous. I got a call from someone telling me where to stand at the Percy speech so that I'd be front and center when that dude walked up to the microphone. Governor Davis' open mic feed appeared in my YouTube account before I knew it was there. As for Senator Jennings' son, I was sent the file an hour before the news conference. Of course I was going to confront him with it and leave it up on my YouTube channel. What a scoop! Still, I'm telling you the truth! You've got to believe me, please!"

Ryan, who's listening in remotely, murmurs, "So, what do you think, Donna?"

"Frankly, I think he's telling the truth."

Arnie looks up from Chuck's computer. "He is, from the looks of things. The YouTube videos were uploaded from a different ISP than the one assigned to this computer. There was a call on his cell phone's caller ID scroll that came in the day of Senator Percy's speech. It's anonymous. So is his next scoop, via text message. Unfortunately, all it says is, 'Assassination will leave a nation in tears. tick-tock, tick-tock.' Maybe Emma can tap into the cell phone provider to see if I can track the source."

"I'm on it," she says over our ear buds.

"Ryan, what would you suggest we do with Chuck?" I ask.

"If we share Arnie's reconnaissance with the NSA, its

investigators will realize they have no cause to indict Chuck under First Amendment standing. And quite frankly, if his source doesn't know he's squealed, it's better to keep Chuck as a decoy, seeing how Arnie's Trojan may lead us right to whoever is sabotaging the candidates. The NSA will certainly appreciate our hard work, and their fingerprints won't be anywhere near it."

"Ironic, isn't it? All this time we thought the candidates would be dodging real bullets. Instead, it's their characters that are being assassinated."

"We're not out of the woods yet, Donna. With Percy out of the way, Congresswoman Catherine Martin, his strongest party opponent, has surged in the polls. She'll be in town tomorrow to meet with some of her biggest donors, and for a couple of photo ops."

"Gotcha. So many candidates, so little time."

Another swipe on the lips with Cherry Noir, and Chuck is sleeping like a baby. When he wakes up, he'll think he had a bad nightmare, and that will be that.

I let the boys dress him. As we're dragging him into the garage, Arnie turns to me and says, "Oh, by the way, I haven't gotten around to assessing your PTA volunteer wheel, but I was able to tap into Hilldale Middle's voting records. You were right. Someone tampered with the tally. It doesn't add up to the paper ballots. I sent Jeff a printout."

"Thanks for doing that, Arnie."

"No problem. That's one smart kid. Who knew he took his politics so seriously."

"Yes, I'm very proud of him. He's got a strong sense of honesty."

"You know what they say: the nut doesn't fall far from the tree."

"I'll take that as a compliment." Better he follow after me than Carl.

If and when the time comes that I break the news to him about his real father, will he feel I've been fair to him, too?

I'll have to convince him that what I did was right.

Not only for him, but for Jack.

And for me, too.

9

Pork Barrel

The political act of pushing through an unnecessary law that benefits a politician's local district, usually to gain favor with local voters.

The term dates from the days when salted pork was occasionally handed out to slaves from large barrels, since the mad rush of politicians to get their district's share of treasury funds looked like that of hungry slaves to the pork barrel.

Don't be such a snob in presuming you're above pork barrel politics. Every time you make your husband's favorite meal in return for extra pin money, you've got pork on your paws. And no one could ever accuse you of finessing your bedside manner in order to get him to fold on your request that he take you to the next Nicholas Sparks tearjerker, am I right?

Yeah, thought so.

Sausage and Cheese Biscuits (From Jana Anthoine, Dunwoody, Georgia)

Ingredients

- 3 cups Bisquik
- 2 cups of your favorite sharp cheese, grated
- 1 pound of sausage, raw

Directions

1. Mix all the ingredients thoroughly, by hand, or you can use a mixer with a dough attachment.
2. Form into one-inch balls.
3. Place each on a cookie sheet, then bake in a pre-heated oven, at 425 degrees, for 10-12 minutes.
4. If you want to add a little more fire-power, spice up the sausage with Tabasco—but trust me, you won't be able to hold more than two balls in your hand at once! (That's what she said.)

"MY CHEEVER WOULD NEVER CHEAT!" PENELOPE IS IN THE FIRST of the classic Five Stages of Parental Grief: Denial.

"I'm sorry, Mrs. Bing, but the evidence is overwhelming to the contrary." Principal Belding points down to the paper ballots, which sit alongside Arnie's timeline for when changes were made to the ballot data entry, which lead directly to the ISP address of Cheever's laptop. After signing onto his personal school cloud account, he took a lucky guess that Miss Bliss's computer password was GARFIELD, her cat's name.

With Cheever as your child, the bumpy road to anger is well traveled. Penelope screeches into that stage at full speed. She slaps him on the back of the head. "How could you shame me like this? If word gets out that you've cheated, we'll both be ruined!"

That's just the point. With all the gotcha moments I've witnessed this week, I wouldn't wish another walk of shame on anyone, not even Penelope's bratty kid.

Cheever buries his head in his chest and mumbles, "I'm sorry, Mom. I … I just wanted you to be proud of me."

It always boils down to that.

Those whose moms love them unconditionally don't reek from the sweat of desperation, as Cheever does now. Then again, he rarely changes his underwear, so maybe that's why he smells. In any regard, I can only imagine that having Penelope as a mother hasn't been easy for the poor kid.

Time to move Penelope into stage three, bargaining. "Principal Belding, I know I speak for Jeff when I say we'd hate for the consequence to outlive the crime."

"Not me," Jeff mutters, "I want him scarred for life."

"That said," I continue, "Perhaps it would be better if Cheever publicly resigned. He can give an interview to Hilldale Middle School's newspaper, the *HMS Pinafore*, stating that, quote, his first priority is to his academic workload, and therefore he'll be stepping down as sixth grade class president, throwing his full support behind his worthy opponent, Jeff Stone, etcetera, etcetera, unquote. It allows him to save face"—I catch Jeff's eye—"and a dear friendship, too."

Jeff glares at me—until he hears Cheever's very loud sigh of relief.

At least, I hope it was a sigh, and not a fart. Just in case, I hold my breath.

Not Jeff. Long ago he accepted his friend's personality flaws, as well as his unchecked bodily functions. The boys shake hands.

"I can live with that, although I'm sure Miss Bliss will want his Civics grade to reflect his actions. If I were you, Cheever, I'd shoot for an A, so that you can at least make a C."

As Penelope and I follow the boys out the door, she mutters, "I suppose you're expecting some quid pro quo."

The remark freezes me in my tracks. "What do you mean by that?"

"Oh, quit acting so innocent, Donna. I know you'd love to tell everyone the real reason why Cheever is resigning."

"If that were my endgame, why did I save your son's skin just now?"

"So, what you're telling me is that you aren't looking for some favor in return—like, say, taking you off lunchroom duty?"

"What? No! ... I mean, unless you want to do it as a way to thank me."

"Ha! Thought so! You're attempting to blackmail me!"

That's it. I've had enough of her psychotic suspicions.

"For the record, Penelope, you brought up the lunchroom, not me. Unlike your son, I play by the book, and accept the hand dealt to me."

Her smile is much too serene. "Good! Friday is your volunteer day, so don't forget your hairnet," she says as she breezes out the front door.

I've never strangled someone with a hairnet, but there's a first time for everything.

THE EMAIL FROM THE HILLDALE PUBLIC LIBRARY READS:

"Another patron has accidentally picked up *The Candidate,* the movie you reserved for this week. However, he has offered to let you pick it up from his house today at 2:00pm promptly ...."

The address follows, as well as a cipher with the candidate's name embedded in it.

After deciphering it, I let out a low, slow whistle when I see where we're to rendezvous with the target.

Jack looks up from the bed. He's been tapping away on his laptop all evening. I'm sure it has something to do with his obsessive research into Lee Chiffray. Except for the real estate connection, he hasn't been able to find anything else that ties Lee with the Quorum. "Don't leave me in suspense."

"I just received a cipher about our next candidate, Massachusetts Congresswoman Catherine Martin. We are to meet her for a face-to-face debriefing, in less than three hours, at the home of one of her largest donors—Lion's Lair."

"Lee Chiffray's place?" He puts down his laptop.

"Well, technically, Babette's—but yes."

"This just in: Technically, Lion's Lair is an asset of Breck International. And since that company has been absorbed by Lee Chiffray's Canadian-based corporation—Global World Industries—she is no longer the owner."

"Wow! I wonder if she realizes it."

Jack chuckles. "If anything can drive a wedge between a gold digger and her latest sugar daddy, it's finding out that he's talked her out of one of her shiny little baubles."

"I don't want to be in the room when she finds out."

He smiles. "Then I guess that means you won't mind if I break the news to her."

Unfortunately, I see where he's going with this. "Go for it … Um, no, don't go for it! I think you know what I mean."

"Of course I do! You mean, 'Do your best to ensure Babette has reasons to doubt Lee is working in her best inter- est. That way, when she's angry enough, she'll feed us the information we're looking for.'"

"I couldn't have said it better—except for the 'do your best' part. 'Your best' is not something I'm willing to share with anyone. Heck, even 'your worst' is better than most."

"Excuse me? I only have a 'best.'" He frowns. "If there is some skill set you find lacking, please be specific."

"Tell you what, let's do a thorough head-to-toe assess- ment, right now."

"I'm always up for that."

I look down at the blanket. "*Mmmm*, yes, so I see. Gee, I wonder where I put my score pad."

He won't let me out of the bed, so I'll have to keep the points in my head:

Okay, yes, the gentleness with which his hands caress me all over earns him a quick ten points;

I'll give him another ten, because he has me undressed in under a minute, flat.

All the while, his fingers tweak and nudge and stroke and taunt my most tender places (9.5 points … Oh, wait— that … felt … *awesome*. Raise it to 10 … plus one … make it two.)

And his tongue gets *very* high marks for creativity. Wow …

I'm …

Speech …

Less ….

Only one item can be measured quantitatively, and at eight and three quarters, it is an impressive specimen. But as we all know firsthand, it is execution that counts most. It would be trite to say that Jack rises to the occasion because he does so much more than that—

In so many different, ways:

Gently—

Robustly—

Wantonly—

Deeply—

Until we are both limp with bliss.

"How am I doing so far?" Jack gasps.

I wait until I've caught my breath to whisper, "Oh, I'm so sorry, I lost track of your points! But please feel free to start over."

I can always count on his competitive spirit.

"Donna, my sweet! Long time no see!" Babette's air kiss misses me by a mile.

Not so with Jack. He turns his head so quickly that her lips miss his, catching his shirt collar instead.

Babette shrugs. "What a shame! You've got my lipstick on your collar. At least this is one time Donna has no excuse to be jealous, since she witnessed my innocent attempt to kiss you."

"Donna doesn't get jealous, she gets even," he assures her.

I love this man.

While Babette lets this sink in, Lee walks out of the estate's grand salon. Seeing us, his face lights up with a smile. "Ah, the Stones! Glad to see the DNC took my advice, and hired your firm for Catherine's protection—and that of the other candidates, of course. I was so impressed by the way in which you exposed Fantasy Island's questionable management practices. It allowed my company to clean house, and to reassess the island's investment potential."

Jack takes my hand and presses my palm as a warning to let him take the lead. "What company is that, again?"

What a smart ass.

"Why Global World Industries, of course." Lee smirks. "But you already know that, don't you? My sources told me Acme was asking around about me, too."

"Well, then certainly thanks are in order—especially for keeping our covers under wraps at the time, since our presence there wasn't supposed to be known to the island's management group." Jack puts out his hand.

Lee shakes it. "Certainly, it was to GWI's advantage to do so. While you investigated Mr. Bourke, I had you investigated, and learned about Acme's dealings with governments all over the world. Bourke's belief that your financial bid was real worked to GWI's advantage as well. I felt it best not to intrude on your discovery process—that is, until Mrs. Stone's life was in peril." He puts his hand on my arm. "Then of course, I did my best to intercede."

The memory of being prey for Fantasy Island's Hunt Club has bile creeping up my throat—especially when I was under the impression that Carl was stalking me.

"All's well that ends well. You got Donna back safely. And a WPI asset was saved from a public relations disaster. Not to mention the incident brought us together. And to think you already knew Babette! Small world, isn't it? But no more unpleasant trips down memory lane! Come meet the candidate I hope will soon be our next president. Catherine is just dying to meet you."

I GUESS WE SHOULD FEEL GUILTY THAT WE WERE DISTRACTED FOR the past few hours while we should have been reading Congresswoman Catherine Martin's dossier, but we aren't. From what we've seen thus far, research gathered from fawning magazine articles aren't worth the bytes they're pixeled on.

One quantifiable fact that is hard to dispute: should she win, besides having the distinction of being the youngest candidate ever to run for the US presidency, she would certainly be the most photogenic, too.

At least the first page in Catherine Martin's dossier explains why she's much more than just a pretty face. Despite being just three years older than me, her twelve-year tenure in the US House of Representatives has made her a strong voice on a few key Congressional committees, such as Armed Forces, Energy, Intelligence, and Foreign Affairs. Having graduated Harvard as a linguist, she is also fluent in French, German, and Chinese.

Despite the flurry of campaign staffers buzzing about, the congresswoman doesn't wait for a formal introduction. Instead, she welcomes me with a warm handshake. "You must be Mrs. Stone. May I call you Donna?"

"Yes, and this is my husband, who is also on your detail."

"Carl, isn't it?" She takes his hand as well. "A pleasure. Lee has been singing your praises. Considering the threats I've received, I now know I'm in good hands."

"How have these threats come to you, and when?" Jack asks.

"Via cell texts and emails. It concerns me that any potential assassin may have obtained access to such confidential information!" She shudders. "They began just in the last couple of weeks, when it was publicly announced that we'd be coming back to California. I'm to receive the Zero Hunger America Humanitarian Award. We thought we'd make the most of the trip. Tomorrow through the early afternoon I'm doing the usual meet-and-greets and photo ops, then in the late afternoon, I'm to be interviewed for a spread in *Mommy Dearest* magazine. The following day, it's been arranged for my husband, Robert, and I to take our son, Evan, to Disneyland. The award will be presented to me later that evening. But the day after is devoted to family. Robert and I want to take Evan to see the houses where we grew up."

I smile. "Oh? You're native Californians?"

"Yes, from Pasadena, in fact."

I do a double-take. "Small world. I'm from there, too."

"Really?" She takes a hard look at me. "Robert and I are both graduates of East Pasadena High."

"So am I." We're around the same age, and yes she does seem familiar to me—

"My maiden name is Connelly. And Bobby was big man on campus—"

Connelly …

Catherine …

CeeCee?

My heart drops into my stomach so quickly that I feel faint.

No. Oh, hell no—

Not CeeCee Connelly.

But yes, now I realize it is the same CeeCee whose back-yard butted up against mine and whose always-open window gave me a peek as to what was to come when I skidded into the very fast teen lane of life.

She let me wear her lipstick, taught me how to use mascara, and showed me how to stuff my bra.

She was supposed to be my sitter. Instead she was my provocateur, nudging me into the forbidden world of gossip, flirtation, and sexual exploration.

In return, I was her confidante, her little sister—

And sadly, the target of her wrath when she so wrongly presumed I threatened her.

How could I, when in fact I idolized her—

When I wanted to be her?

Because of some pathetic misunderstanding, so long ago, over—

"Donna? My God, is that you?"

When I turn around, I *see him*:

Bobby.

Tall, blond and tanned, with a twinkle in his eye and a teasing grin on his lips.

But how can that be? Like me, he should have grown older—not to mention wiser, and perhaps more contrite for the cruel slights administered to others.

To me.

He sees me staring at him. And yet, ever so polite, he holds out his hand. "Hello, my name is Evan Martin."

I take it, and hope that he doesn't realize my palm is sweaty.

Or that my heart is stuck in my throat.

The heart he broke into sad little bits, so long ago.

But this boy is not Bobby. I know this because Bobby stands behind the son who is his spitting image.

The real Bobby is older, with a few gray hairs and a few more pounds. The creases around Real Bobby's mouth are deeper, and there is a tiny web of wrinkles by his eyes, which almost disappear as they open from his shock at seeing me.

Do I look the same to him? I'm sure I don't. I'm certainly a few inches taller than my eleven-year-old self, hopefully not as scrawny, and certainly happier, despite the path that has led me here, back to them.

To protect CeeCee.

CeeCee who is now staring hard at me through cold eyes; whose smile falters, and whose voice cracks under the weight of her wariness from some unknown threat:

Me.

But today my role is not to inflict wounds. Instead, I must serve and protect—

My very first enemy:

CeeCee Connelly, who now goes by Catherine Martin or Mrs. Robert Martin.

She is now Bobby's wife.

So instead of crying in front of him, or berating him for hurting me so long ago, or showing anyone—especially CeeCee—that I can't separate some long-buried hurt from my official duties, I smile and feign memory loss. "Um …

I'm sorry. I mean, yes, my name is Donna, but do I know you?"

The pupils of Bobby's eyes flicker like a camera shutter right at the moment in which its film is exposed to light, preserving forever the reality of life at that very moment:

Bobby is married to CeeCee, and I am no more than a bodyguard paid by the political party that wishes for her to win the upcoming election.

I wonder why is there so much sadness in his eyes.

10

Kitchen Cabinet

A politician's "kitchen cabinet" is a group of unofficial advisers who are considered to be unduly influential to his or her decision-making process.

This can include a campaign manager, a spouse, mentors and previous professors, and those renowned for their knowledge and skills in the areas of important policies: finance, foreign affairs, and domestic issues, such as education and health care.

Since these confidants are not elected officials in their own right, those whose lives are being affected by the politician in question can only hope that his kitchen cabinet members (a) aren't just kiss-ass sycophants; (b) haven't filled the candidate's coffers to the extent that he is now their lapdog; and (c) that their opinions don't confuse him to the point that he always chooses the recommendation of the last person who has talked to him, a.k.a., the "last one in the elevator" syndrome.

More than likely, one of these scenarios will play out, so be prepared to feel disenfranchised. Hey, there's always the next election, and the next candidate.

And the next kitchen cabinet influencing decisions on your behalf.

One thing everyone can agree upon is that a pie is only as great as its crust. That said, this recipe is tried-and-true to create a crisp, flaky crust every time:

The Pie Lady's Crust (From Kristin Isaacson, Seattle, Washington)

Ingredients

- 2 cups sifted flour
- ¾ tsp. salt and 1 TBS sugar
- ½ cup Crisco
- ¼ cup butter
- 4-6 TBS ice water

Directions

1. Sift together flour, salt and sugar.
2. Add Crisco, and blend with a pastry blender until it is the consistency of meal.
3. Add the butter, and cut into the Crisco/flour mixture, until it is the size of peas.
4. Add ice water, one tablespoon at a time, stirring

lightly with a butter knife until dough starts to
form (don't be worried if the dough gets a
little wet).

5. Divide into halves, and roll onto a generously
   floured surface.

6. Remember to own your dough—and don't let it
   own you!

"MOM, BABETTE CHIFFRAY CALLED JUST A FEW MINUTES AGO."
Mary disdainfully plucks black olives off the pizza Aunt
Phyllis has ordered for everyone, including Wendy, who is
busy scraping mushrooms off her piece, then the girls
swap piles.

It saddens me to see that Babs is not here, too. All week
long, Mary has been ignoring my seemingly innocent questions about her friend's wellbeing.

"Did Mrs. Chiffray leave a message?" I ask.

"She said something about a change of plans. You'll need
to be at her house at least by eight-fifteen tomorrow, so that
you can accompany Congresswoman Martin to her first
campaign stop."

Wendy looks up from patting down her olives. "Are you
really part of the congresswoman's entourage?"

I sigh. "Not really."

Jack nudges and mutters, "Tell them the truth."

I nudge him back. "Yes. Well, really I'm helping out your

father, whose firm has some dealings with her campaign. She's here with her husband and her son—"

"Oh my God!" Wendy squeals. "Someone said they spotted Evan Martin jogging in the park; so it's true! He's here! He is *such* a hottie!"

Yes, he is his father's son.

I turn my face so that Jack can't see my frustration. Too late. I catch his frown in the mirror.

Wendy nudges Mary, who then very nonchalantly asks, "How long is Evan—I mean, are the Martins, in town?"

Whatever scheme they're hatching is going to be nipped in the bud, right here and now. "Not long at all. Just a couple of days, in fact. The congresswoman has a few events, then she and her husband are stopping in Pasadena, where they grew up—"

I stop short, but it's too late. Aunt Phyllis looks up. "Our home town? Do we know the family?"

Okay, here it comes. "Yes. In fact, Catherine's maiden name is Connelly. She's—"

"Not your old pal, CeeCee Connelly," Aunt Phyllis exclaims.

"Yep, the one and the same," Jack says.

Aunt Phyllis lets that sink in. "Well, what do you know? So I guess you two will be as thick as thieves again, now that she's here."

I toss my pizza onto my plate. "Trust me—we were never 'thick as thieves.'"

She's laughing so hard, she almost chokes on her pizza.

"I'll say you were! I remember the time I caught you trying to climb out of your window in the middle of the night, because CeeCee was tossing pebbles at it. And then there was that incident when she wrote a note to your teacher as if it came from your mother, so that you could get out of class and play hooky. Boy, your father was hot under the collar when he found out about that one—"

"Aunt Phyllis, please, you're exaggerating!" My warning comes much too late. The girls are staring at me, as if I'm some sort of exotic creature they've never seen before.

Yes, I was young once. Yes, I did things that were sometimes silly, and other times stupid.

And yes, I made mistakes I'll always live to regret.

And so will you.

Hopefully, you'll be able to forgive yourself for them.

As for those who led you down the path of temptation, they have their own memories to deal with, their own hells to answer for.

The thought of me doing all the things I've warned her against has Mary collapsing in a fit of giggles. Laughter, especially at the expense of others, is a slippery slope. Wendy also caves in, as does Aunt Phyllis. Not to be left out, Trisha giggles, too, as if it's the funniest joke she's ever heard.

Jeff shouts from the great room for all of us to "KEEP IT DOWN, ALREADY!" Since his own election, he's been hooked on *PBS Newshour*'s primary coverage.

Shields and Brooks have much to talk about. With the

candidates' campaigns sinking under the weight of their past deeds, one can only guess who'll be last man—or woman—standing.

My bet is on CeeCee.

For all the wrong reasons.

Finally, Mary gets her giggles under control. "Mom, since you're hanging with your old friend, do you mind if I interview her for the school newspaper? We're each supposed to choose a candidate and write a biography, but a one-on-one interview will give me an instant A."

Wendy shoves her. "Oh, I am so jealous! You'll be interviewing Catherine Martin!"

"Wait—Mom knows Congresswoman Martin?" All of a sudden, we have Jeff's attention. "Mom, can I interview her, too? Please? Miss Bliss would flip out if I got the chance—"

"I asked first," Mary growls at him. "Right, Mom? If anyone is going to interview her, it's me—"

"No one is interviewing anyone—least of all, Catherine Martin!" I'm loud enough—and angry enough—that they all get the message.

Everyone shuts up.

Everyone is confused.

Jack, especially, who turns to Aunt Phyllis and says, "We're going to take the dogs out for a walk."

Then he grabs my hand, and pulls me out the door after him.

He doesn't realize that I need more than a bit of fresh air.

I need to forget the past.

"WANT to tell me what happened between you and CeeCee?"

Jack is hanging upside down by his knees on the playground jungle gym. From that position, he pulls himself up, doing a series of crunches that are impressive, and explain why he's the only man in the neighborhood with six-pack abs worth sighing over.

Okay, now that Dominic lives here, too, Jack has a little competition, which at least gives me one reason to be glad he's moved to town.

Where do I start? I wonder.

As if reading my mind, he says, "From the beginning."

With that, it spills out of me: all the memories, all the angst, all the grief and regrets.

All the shame of trying to be normal under extraordinary circumstances.

"I didn't know my mother was dying," I start. "All I knew was that CeeCee Connelly, the older girl who lived behind us, liked me enough to hang with me."

He nods slowly. "How old were you at the time?"

"I was eleven, almost twelve. I'd just started sixth grade. CeeCee was fourteen."

"So you were in middle school, and she was in high school."

"Yes, at the time, she was a freshman in high school. I thought it odd at first. I mean, all that time we'd lived so close, but she'd ignored me. You remember how it is when you're a teenager. The last thing you want to do is hang with kids who are younger. Anyway, she started coming around—you know, to hang out, to talk. Friendly as can be. Of course, I was flattered. CeeCee was just as she is now: the queen bee. Truly, between middle school and high school, she blossomed into this gorgeous young woman, and all the boys fell over themselves to find out who she was—especially Bobby."

"You mean, Robert Martin."

"Yes. He was sixteen—a junior. And I'm sure he got razzed for falling so hard for a freshman, but he didn't care. He knew she had something special. We all knew it." I try hard to swallow the lump in my throat. "I guess that should have been the tip-off that the last thing CeeCee Connelly would do is hang with a skinny, pimply sixth-grader."

"So, why did she?"

I bite my lip. "It was my mother's idea, although neither my dad nor I knew it at the time. Mother had already gotten her cancer diagnosis from her doctor. She knew she'd be 'napping' a lot, what with the drugs she'd be taking, and with the disease eating away at her. She wanted someone to watch over me—and to distract me. CeeCee was someone she knew I'd look up to. So, she paid CeeCee to come over in the afternoons, to watch me while Mother 'ran her errands.'" I wipe away a tear. "You see, she didn't want a caretaker for herself, she wanted one for me. All the time I thought she was shopping or at her bridge club, she was getting chemo, or being poked and prodded by her doctors. Sometimes she'd just nap in her bedroom."

He hikes himself off the monkey bars and eases himself onto the slide. "Was CeeCee mean to you?"

"No … Well, not at first. We did our homework together. She showed me how to wear my clothes—you know, roll my skirt at the waist, and unbutton the top two buttons of my blouse, so that I didn't look like such a little dork. She taught me how to put on make-up. Once, she even cut my hair. I was like—I imagined I was her little sister." I shrug. "Eventually she'd open up to me about her other friends. Unlike the other girls her age, I wasn't jealous of her. I idolized her! She could see that. I guess it's easy to talk to someone who is in awe of you, and who will cross-her-heart-and-hope-to-die before revealing any secret you tell her."

"When did things change between you?"

"When Bobby started hanging around." When I close my eyes, I see his face as it was then. "He was gaga over her. She loved it. Of course, he was just as handsome as Evan is now. But he was smart, too. It doesn't surprise me that he's been so successful with all of his Internet start-ups. He was voted Most Likely to Succeed for a reason." I pause. "Soon, he knew her routine, and made a point to walk by my house. CeeCee made sure we were always on the front porch. She'd ignore him, but he always found a way to invite himself up. I'd sit in awe as she flirted with him. Once, she sent me inside to pour lemonade. I was walking out with it when I saw them, through the window: kissing. I was too embarrassed to interrupt them, so I waited until they came up for air. By then, my arms were aching, from holding the tray."

Jack chuckles in the hope that I will, too.

But I can't, because my heart is beating too hard in my chest. "I was fascinated. I felt I was watching my future, my destiny, through them—and that they let me in on it because they thought I was cool, too. I had no idea that CeeCee was paid to hang out with me, or that it gave her the added convenience of seeing Bobby without her own mother knowing about it." I sigh. "Soon I was fantasizing that it was me in Bobby's arms—that he was making out with me, not her."

"When did she catch on?"

"She caught me writing his name with mine, inside of a heart. When she saw how embarrassed I was, she laughed, and said she thought it was adorable. But I was mortified—even more so when she told Bobby about it, in front of me."

"Did he laugh, too?"

"Oddly, no. Whereas other boys would have probably said something cruel about it, I think he knew I was embarrassed and he said, 'I'll keep it in mind. She's going to be a knock-out when she grows up.'"

"He was right."

Jack's declaration lifts a smile from me. "I appreciate you saying so—and I certainly was flattered he thought so, too. But CeeCee wasn't too happy about it. She huffed off. A couple of days later they made up—in fact, they made out in my bedroom. But things were never the same between CeeCee and me."

"What about between you and Bobby?"

Can he see me blushing in the dark? "One night—I found out later that my father knew my mother's prognosis by then, and my parents stayed overnight at the hospital, for tests—CeeCee was to spend the night with me. She used it as an excuse for a party. She invited over two girlfriends, and of course Bobby came over with two other boys. They played games. You know, Spin the Bottle, that sort of thing. One of the boys suggested that I play, too. I didn't want to, but CeeCee insisted on it. 'You're going to do it sooner or later, so you might as well do it with people who aren't dorky middle-schoolers,' was how she put it."

"That was cruel of her to say."

"Oh, it gets better, believe me." I take a deep breath. "The game is called 'Seven Minutes in Heaven.'"

"I know it. Boy plus girl plus a room with a bed, behind a locked door." He shakes his head.

"Exactly." I shudder. "We used my bedroom. Each girl would pull the name of a boy out of a hat. I went last. The sounds behind my bedroom door freaked me out, but because I wanted to impress CeeCee, I kept my cool. But then … then it was my turn. I don't remember the boy's name now. All I remember is that he was big and bulky and made all kinds of dirty remarks to the other girls. When he heard his name, he snickered and high-fived the other boy. Then he jerked me by my arm toward my bedroom. I didn't like the look in his eye and I began to panic, but he wouldn't let me go. He held me around my waist and practically threw me onto my little twin bed. I fought hard, and the tears were falling so fast that I couldn't see what was happening. Maybe that was a good thing, because I could feel his hand slip under my tee-shirt.

At the same time, he was grinning like a mad jack-o-lantern … And then …"

Jack squeezes my hand. "What happened?"

"He wasn't there anymore. Bobby had pulled him off and was pummeling the guy, and CeeCee was screaming at him. When he stopped, the other boy was bleeding all over. He scrambled out of there, and so did the other kids, even CeeCee."

"You spent the night, alone?"

"No. Bobby stayed there—on the couch. But when he was trying to make me stop crying, he held me. And … he kissed me."

The thought weighs heavy on my lids, pushing them down. But in the darkness behind my eyes, the memory plays before me, as if I'm watching an old movie:

Bobby is holding me, shushing me—

Kissing me.

On the cheek.

Until I turn toward him, so that his lips are on mine.

But just for a second—

One very sweet moment.

Maybe longer.

When he pulls away, he is breathing heavy, and I am, too. Then he says, "I'm with CeeCee."

"But why?" I ask. What I mean to add is, *when you can be with me.*

"Because she is who I love. She is my everything. She is the queen of the universe."

His universe. A place in which I don't exist, and never have.

That's my cue—to scramble away, to pretend it never happened.

But I don't. If anyone is going to walk away, it will be him.

He gets up and goes to the couch.

"Donna, he didn't—" Jack's voice brings me back to the here and now.

"You mean … No! Quite the opposite, Jack, believe me. It was all very innocent. Even back then, he was very much in love with CeeCee." I sigh. "But because he didn't walk out with her, she thought the worst, too. Soon, the rumors were flying. I was a bad girl. I was no longer a virgin. At the same time, my parents broke the news to me that my mother didn't have long to live. I became her caretaker. Thank goodness, it gave me the excuse I needed to take a leave of absence from school. Until Aunt Phyllis came over from the East Coast to live with us, I left my mother's side only twice a week—for a grocery run, and to meet with my teacher after school, to get my homework and turn in the assignments from the previous week." I shrug. "One day, as I was walking home, Bobby was waiting for me. He said he needed to talk to me. I knew it was CeeCee who had started the rumors, so of course I had nothing to say to him. But he insisted. He wanted to apologize. He said he, too, knew she was the source of the gossip, but that if anyone asked, he always denied anything happened. I wanted to believe him. And I asked him to kiss me, one last time."

I still remember the sweetness of his lips.

And the shame in his eyes.

"I was with him at the most a half-hour. When I got home, CeeCee was there, sitting with mother, as if nothing had happened! I was surprised—shocked, really. But when CeeCee rose to leave, Mother called her by my name. I was heartbroken. I felt it was yet another of CeeCee's cruel jokes, and I told her to get out of our house and leave us alone. She told me I was overreacting and laughed at me. It only made me angrier. It felt great to open the door and tell her to get the hell out." I tremble at the memory. "When I got back into my mother's room, she asked me if I'd 'made the pie.' I didn't know what she was talking about! With her medications, she sometimes said things that didn't make sense. But later, when I went into the kitchen, I saw that her recipe tin was open. Her special apple pie recipe was missing."

"CeeCee had taken it?"

I nod. "Yes! Can you believe it?"

"She's a politician. I'd believe anything." He laughs as he pulls me out of the swing and into his arms. "I love your apple pie."

"You should. It's my mother's recipe. Thank goodness I'd memorized it." I shrug. "I guess it's CeeCee's now, too. I've no doubt it's the one she used as her entry in the county fair —and as her 'hobby' for the Tip Top Teen USA contest." I shrug. "I'm glad to see she's too busy to use it anymore. And on that note—"

I reach for my cell phone.

"Who are you calling?" Jack asks.

I grin. "My old friend, Congresswoman Catherine

Martin. She owes me a favor. Payback is an interview with Mary."

He laughs. "She's getting off easy."

"You can say that again! She's lucky it's not with Brenda Stark, in Dominic's torture grotto."

The dogs leap as we kiss, but we don't care.

Fate played me one winning card. I ended up with my dream man after all.

11

Fishing Expedition

An investigation with no pre-determined purpose, often by one political party seeking damaging information about another. Such inquiries are likened to fishing because they pull up whatever they happen to catch.

You're probably adept at fishing expeditions, and never realized it. For example, when you ask your husband supposedly innocent questions about his business trips or his nights out with his pals, any and all information (or for that matter, fibs) can be used against him at a later date—either in the bedroom, or in a court of law.

Speaking of a great catch, here's a wonderful way to serve salmon! Try it with this unique topping combination:

Black Bean Salmon (Compliments of SamTheCookingGuy.com)

Ingredients

- 1/2 cup apricot preserves (which is pretty much the same as jam)
- 1/4 cup black bean & garlic sauce
- 1 whole salmon filet, about 1.5 pounds, skin off might be easier
- 3 green onions, finely chopped
- Sesame seeds

Directions

1. Heat broiler to high.
2. Put salmon on a baking sheet covered lightly with oil.
3. Combine apricot jam and black bean sauce in a small bowl - mix well and spread on top of salmon to cover.
4. Broil 4-5 inches from heat, approximately 7 minutes for each inch of thickness.
5. Remove to a platter or serving plates and sprinkle with green onions and sesame seeds – serve.

IT'S BEEN ONE HELL OF A MORNING.

Besides the usual throngs of awed and adoring voters, Congresswoman Catherine Martin was met with tomatoes thrown by protestors who take issue with her vote to cut farm subsidies.

She ducked, and I leaped, taking them in her stead.

Then there was the bowl of borscht tossed at her, from someone upset over the speech poo-pooing UN sanctions against Russia for its human rights violations. I pushed her out of the way just in the nick of time, only to get soaked.

Dominic nodded approvingly. "You look great in red. Thank goodness it's a cold soup. Otherwise, you'd have been scalded—especially around the Bristol region, since that took the brunt … Oh my! Perhaps you'd like to borrow my coat."

I look down to see what he's staring at.

Hmmm. Cold tomato soup on a sheer blouse equals nipples standing at attention. In other words, not a great look.

I leave my Acme team to go home and change clothes. Mary is out of school now, so she rides back with me. We catch up with Catherine's entourage just as she's wrapping up a speech with the local chapter of the League of Women Voters.

Mary listens, enraptured, as Catherine regales the crowd with her vision of America at its best. In it, employment is at its peak, and our nation of producers is rewarded with high wages and real benefits. Higher education is for everyone who wishes to take advantage of it. Teachers are paid hand-somely for educating our nation's best and brightest. Which of us doesn't fit that description?

If only we saw ourselves as others see us.

In Catherine's new world order, the safety and security of our citizens will always be a top priority. "We've already paid too high a price, forfeited too many lives, to go back on this promise," she vows.

Mary's iPhone captures it all on video. I'm sure it also picks up Mary's declaration, "I want to be just like her."

For once, I hope my daughter does not get her wish.

"I'M SO HAPPY YOUR DAUGHTER WAS INTERESTED IN accompanying us this afternoon," Catherine says sweetly. "My goodness, what a pretty little thing she is! She reminds me of you at that age."

"Do you really think so? I can't imagine you'd remember me at fourteen. You dumped me as a friend before I was twelve." I'm trying to keep the edge out of my voice, but my guess is that I'm failing miserably.

I know this to be the case when Catherine, responds, "Yes, I think you're right! I'm sure it was your colorful reputation I remember. My God, who could forget it? I didn't—not for years."

Before I can say another word, she glides away, greeting *Mommy Dearest*'s publisher, Allison O'Connor, with air kisses.

I am left standing with a mob of fawning acolytes.

After what I divulged to Jack last night, I'm glad he's not here to see her imperious diss.

Unfortunately, Mary does, and it embarrasses her enough that she turns her head in order to hide her mortification.

I can't say that I blame her. From what she's seen and heard thus far, Catherine is not only the dream candidate, but a great wife, mother, and issues-oriented candidate. In fact, on the limo ride here, Catherine graciously answered Mary's long list of carefully thought-out questions, piercing my daughter with the gaze she reserves for the likes of Katie Couric, Anderson Cooper and Oprah. The staff adviser to Hilldale High School's newspaper, the*Signal*, will run the interview on the front page, which thrills Mary to no end.

Now, if only her mother doesn't ruin it for her.

Okay, I'll be on my best behavior, from now on out.

I've allowed my mind to wander while the interview hits its stride. On the other hand, Mary sits quietly in a corner of the studio, scribbling away on her pad. I presume she's comparing the magazine publisher's questions to the ones she asked in the limo, and is taking special note of Catherine's seemingly thoughtful answers.

She doesn't realize that Catherine has spent a lifetime answering these very same questions, and that she's had years to hone her answers to them. Every tilt of the head, every pause, and every inflection is well practiced.

Robert and Evan, who sit quietly on either side of Catherine, wear the placid smiles that go hand in hand with a life spent reluctantly in the spotlight. I do notice, however, that

Evan's adoring gaze will sometimes drift from his mother to Mary.

Just as Robert's eyes shift my way.

It's a good thing that Jack is with Dominic, covering the studio doors. Otherwise he would have picked up on it, and gotten the wrong idea.

Me? I know better.

Suddenly something the publisher says catches my attention: "—your renowned apple pie recipe! If you don't mind, we'll duplicate it here, right now." Allison's hand sweeps out over the room, where a state-of-the-art kitchen awaits them.

Huh? *Her* recipe?

Catherine blinks twice. This is her *gotcha* moment. My mother's recipe isn't something she ever knew by heart.

Unlike me.

"Ah, what a wonderful—and totally unexpected surprise," Catherine purrs. "But I wouldn't want to muss my suit."

"No problem! We've got a full apron, right here." From behind her chair, Allison pulls out two of them, emblazoned with the magazine's curvy script logo.

Catherine's lips curl into a smile. "How thoughtful." She snaps her fingers for her press secretary Lydia.

While Lydia rushes to her side, I grab my cell phone and call Arnie.

He answers with a "Yo, boss lady, what's up?"

"Quick—you have the code to Congresswoman Martin's iCloud account, right?"

"Yep. I'm still assessing the threats that came to her. Why do you ask?"

"I need to access something in there."

"I'll send it to you now."

A second later I get the code—and I'm in the cloud, searching for the term *Apple Pie.*

Ah, here it is …

My fingers work fast. I delete a cup of sugar. Instead the recipe now calls for sorghum. Forget the pinch of salt. Add three-quarters of a cup. Use crabapples, not Fiji. And the crust will be cornmeal, not flour.

Done.

And so is any future reliance on this recipe by CeeCee Connelly Martin.

Should I warn Mary not to take a bite? Nah. It'll be a great life lesson:

No one is perfect.

It's obvious that neither of these women have cooked a day in their lives. They glare at the editor who dares to question the type of apple or flour or sweetener the recipe calls for, let alone the generous use of salt.

The photo op is priceless. At each step of the process, they stop to wrap their arms around each other and smile wide.

They coo when they pull the baked pie out of the oven and pause for the camera, with forks poised at their mouths.

But the money shot is the look of horror on their faces as they spit out the pie.

The photographer, who is on rote, keeps clicking away, catching every squint, pucker, and gag.

I bite my lip to keep from snorting.

Only Robert doesn't feel the need to hold his tongue or look the other way. He's laughing so hard that the others can't help but join in.

Everyone but Catherine.

Her eyes flash angrily. As if driven by a heat-seeking missile, they seek me out.

I wave back, innocently. But there is no mistaking the message in her glare: *Destroy.*

She stalks off, her advance team in tow.

Evan is looking over Mary's shoulder, reading her notes. When she realizes it, she blushes deeply. He says something that makes her laugh. Her reply has him doubling over.

I feel as if I'm looking at my past.

Robert is watching them, too. I catch his eye. He smiles. Worse yet, he comes up to me.

It would be rude to walk away.

It will break my heart to make chitchat and pretend there was never anything between us.

Then again, maybe there wasn't, and I imagined it all.

"The publisher is suggesting that they reduce the spread to just the interview, and nix the recipe," he says with a chuckle. "But Catherine won't hear of it. She says it's all or nothing. I can't wait to see how she spins this one."

Lydia sidles beside him. With a take-no-prisoners tone,

she announces, "The congresswoman is leaving and requests that you join her."

Evan hears her, too. "Dad, do we have to? Can't we just meet up with her later?"

"That's a great idea," he says firmly, all the while looking at Lydia.

She gets the message, loud and clear: Make up some excuse for us.

She frowns at me as she stalks off.

"I'll be glad to give you a lift. Jack and Dominic can accompany the congresswoman."

"Ryan isn't going to like it," Jack and Dominic warn me in unison, through my ear bud.

For once, what Ryan wants isn't my concern.

I've taken off my ear bud, and disengaged my phone.

It's time to go home.

BECAUSE OF EVAN'S PROCLAMATION THAT HE WAS CHEATED OUT of a slice of apple pie, Mary insists on making him one.

"It's the best you'll ever have," she promises. "It's my grandmother's pie recipe."

When he tastes it, he'll never go back to store-bought. Or stolen, for that matter. Now having watched his mother cook, I've no doubt she screwed up Mother's recipe many times before now.

While Mary bakes and Evan flirts and Mary flirts back, Robert meanders from the kitchen into my living room. He picks up a picture of Trisha and Mary, taken this summer, for a formal family portrait. Both are dressed in identical pink sundresses adorned with tiny white rosebuds. "Why do girls always seem happy in that color? It's CeeCee's favorite."

He then strolls over to one of the floor-to-ceiling bookcases. He seems impressed with the depth and breadth of our reading material: Jack's world history and science tomes, my collection of classics and mystery novels. Then he spots something sitting flat on the tallest shelf: one of my high school yearbooks—

It's the one from my freshman year. He reaches it with no problem, and flips through the pages. I'm too far away to see which one stops him. Since it was CeeCee's senior year, I'm sure it's one of the many shots glorifying her reign as the school's queen bee.

"Do you still hate me?" he asks in a soft voice.

"Hate you?" The thought pulls me down into a wingback chair. "No, never! Why in the world would you think that?"

"I …" He shrugs. "I guess it was nothing, really. You may not remember, but we ran into each other once. By then, I was in college and you were a senior in high school. I was home during a holiday break, and I went to catch an East Pasadena basketball game. I came up to you, but you ignored me completely. I thought that, after the letter…never mind."

"I'm sorry, but I don't remember you at one of the games," I murmur.

I'm lying. Of course I do. I could tell he wanted redemption, to talk through his shame. But what was the point? The last thing I needed was for the rumors to start up again.

More importantly, I didn't want to feel for him again.

He buys my blank stare. "Forget I said anything."

There is one thing I can now acknowledge wholeheartedly. "I hated CeeCee. For what she did to my mother."

He snorts. "Your mother? What about for what she did to you?"

"I guess it would have hurt much more if I hadn't lost Mother around the same time. But I didn't have time to think of me. I had to take care of my father, before I lost him, too."

Robert nods. "Yes, I heard he—that he had a hard time of it."

"Everything you heard was right. We both missed her, terribly. He became a drunk. I became … me."

"You seem the same to me," he insists.

I laugh, but I'm not happy to hear that. "Trust me, I'm a much different person than the one you remember." I shrug. "But you haven't changed. You're still in top form. And you and CeeCee—"

He frowns. "There is no 'me and CeeCee.' There is only CeeCee. And then there's Evan and me." He bows his head. "She promised she'd quit Congress after this term. Little did I know that she meant to run for the presidency instead—and hold onto her seat, too, in case she loses the primary." When he sits down, the yearbook is still in his hands.

That's when I notice the page isn't turned to a picture of her. On it is the only picture of me: my class picture. The photographer wanted me to smile, but instead I glared at the camera. I'd lost my mother and my reputation. There was no reason to say cheese. He's lucky I didn't say *fuck you.*

Robert stares down at it and says, "She won't be the next president."

"What? How do you know? I mean, if anything, she's now got a wide open field."

"Because she's a fake, and she's a liar. She has been, all her life. And no matter how many voters she fools, or how much money comes her way, she'll always be just that—"

I laugh. "That sounds like the definition of 'politician' to me."

He laughs, too. Freely. Uncontrollably.

Until he cries.

Until he comes out with it:

"It's over between us," he chokes through his tears.

"No. You're wrong, Bobby. With CeeCee, it's always about you."

"You're wrong, Donna! Somewhere along the way, she quit believing in that—in *us.*" He drops his head on his chest. "The people who own her are dirty. But she doesn't care because doing their bidding will make her the most powerful person in the world." He shrugs.

"Queen of the Universe," I murmur.

"You remember that, do you? Yes, queen of the universe." He sighs heavily. "If only she cared as much about our marriage."

"She's got to! It's what has defined her life, from the beginning. For God's sake, she stole my mother's apple pie recipe over it! She spread rumors about me, because of it! Don't tell me it was all for nothing."

He shakes his head. "Donna, trust me, it's over! There's someone else now—some guy who calls her on a hot pink cell phone. It's not a family phone, or registered with her campaign, or the secure phone for her congressional business."

"Oh." I fall back into the cushions. "Have you asked her about it?"

"Why? So I can hear another one of her lies?" He shakes his head. "I can't stomach what she's become. All I wanted was a normal life—just the two of us, and Evan. "This—right here—could have been us."

Is he right?

If there had been no CeeCee, would Robert have hung around and fallen in love with me?

If my mother hadn't died, would I have been the strong person I am today?

Would I have run into Carl at a shooting range and fallen in love, and married him—only to have him disappear, and for Jack to take his place, both within Acme, and my life?

But Robert loved CeeCee once. There is no denying it.

And no matter my mother's fate, mine put me in the path of Carl, and Jack.

Instead, I say the one thing he needs to hear: "This would not have been us. We were never meant to be any more than this—the closest of friends—always."

He nods because we both know this to be true.

"In any event, I'm asking her for a divorce, after the

awards ceremony tomorrow night." He sounds hollow, soulless. "She'll hate it because it will damage her political career. On the other hand, it may save her—it may save *us*. Maybe she'll be my CeeCee again."

I say nothing. But I hold his hand while he cries.

When his sobs finally subside, he wipes his tears away, nods, and stands up. "I could use a piece of your mother's pie," he says.

It's time to put the past behind us, and live in the present.

It is time for pie.

12

Front Burner

Any issue that must be dealt with immediately is, metaphorically, moved to the front burner of a campaign.

The same thing goes for a relationship, or a family. For example, if you discover your husband is having an affair, you don't sweep the knowledge under the carpet. You confront him with it.

If anything is to be buried, it's his body in the backyard.

Preferably under your rose bushes. Great fertilizer! (Just sayin'.)

While you're at it, plant his harlot there as well.

Speaking of front burners, put this stove-top dish in front of your family, and watch them gobble it up:

Great Tasting Goulash (From Alicia Carmical, of Cabot, Arkansas)

Ingredients

- lb.
- 1 pkg elbow macaroni
- 1 can diced tomatoes with basil, garlic, oregano
- 1/4 cup of ketchup
- 1/2 to 3/4 cup of V8 juice
- 1/2 onion, diced

Directions

1. Fry hamburger and onion until cooked, drain.
2. Cook macaroni, drain.
3. Add all ingredients to the meat, and adjust to taste.

"If you're to continue on this mission, you've got to apologize to Congresswoman Martin," Ryan growls.

"Apologize? For what, pray tell?" Yes, I'm being a brat.

"Where should I start?" he roars. "Wait—I have an idea! Why don't I just read the list sent over by her campaign manager?" I hear him rummaging through his desk. "Okay, let's start with 'insubordination.'"

"What does that mean, exactly?"

"I take it to mean, 'being a smart ass.'"

"Okay, yeah, I can live with that."

"Well, I can't. Nor can I live with 'sabotaging her with a media outlet' or 'kidnapping her family.'"

"Whoa—*so* not true! Bobby and Evan begged me to take them with us—"

"'Bobby?' Who the hell is Bobby? … Oh, you mean *Robert.*"

"It's … an old family nickname. We're close, dear friends."

Ryan mutters, "Donna, you aren't his family. You haven't talked to the man in years. At least, not according to his wife."

I think that one through. Then I whisper, "Ryan, neither you nor Catherine tell me who I am to anyone—especially someone who calls me a close, dear friend."

He gets it.

I know this, because he's silent.

Now it's my turn in our little game of quid pro quo.

"Okay, I'll apologize. What's her number?"

"She wants you to do it in person."

"Where, and when?"

"Lee Chiffray's. She's there now for a meeting with some top donors. I presume I don't have to tell you to behave."

"Of course not."

"Good. Now get over there, before she changes her mind." The next thing I know, I'm listening to a dead phone.

Time to start up the hill, to run the gauntlet of Acme agents who stand sentry from the gate at the street to the circular drive at the front door.

One thing I know for sure: even crow would taste better than Catherine's apple pie.

I SHOULD HAVE FIGURED CATHERINE WOULD KEEP ME WAITING, but come on—two whole hours?

I've been relegated to a hard bench in Lion Lair's two-story foyer. Every now and then the frantic flock of Catherine's minions will scurry by, or a servant will tiptoe down the hall. In any regard, I am ignored, as if I'm part of the ugly flocked wallpaper.

I'm here long enough to pick up on the sounds unique to a house: the creak of footsteps overhead; the whisper of drapes fluttering against an open window—

Or a woman's sob.

Babette.

I slip upstairs, following the sound.

She is sitting in the master suite, on the tuffet in front of her vanity mirror, her head bowed.

I stand there at a loss for words. Despite our intertwined paths and the friendship between Trisha and Janie, we've never been friends, let alone close confidants. That alone is reason enough to turn and leave—

"Donna … please don't go." Her request comes out in a whisper.

I walk back in and sit down on the bed; she turns to face me. "Tell me the truth. Is he having an affair?"

"He … who?"

"Lee, of course! Please be honest with me."

"Babette, I … I hope you don't think that I …"

Her eyes harden. "I said be honest."

"There is nothing going on between Lee and me."

She stares, incredulous.

The next thing I know, she's laughing hysterically.

What the hell?

"Oh, Donna! You can be such a clown! Granted, yes, I needed a good laugh, but I was being dead serious."

Seriously dead? Don't tempt me.

I force my hands to my sides. "Babette, I was being candid. Your husband and I are just friends."

She shrugs. "I know that, silly! Lee wouldn't be caught dead—Oh! Don't be angry! What I meant to say is that you're just not his type."

"Oh?" Ha! If only she knew.

Heck, if only I knew. The man is a conundrum.

"I meant Catherine. You're her bodyguard, so you should know. Are they having an affair?"

"Hell, no! She's running for the presidency, for God's sake! The woman barely has time to take a pee, no less have a quickie in some VA Hall john."

She frowns. "You know, we'd be better friends if you weren't so vulgar."

Well then, thank goodness for my potty mouth.

"Besides," she continues, I think you're wrong. I saw him sneak her that special cell phone—"

"Wait … a cell phone? Was it hot pink?"

She nods. "So you do know!"

"I know she carries one that color, but it couldn't be … well. What I mean is, perhaps it has to do with campaign business. He's in charge of fundraising and vetting her VP candidates. Maybe he's afraid word will get out as to whom she'll be choosing."

"My God, you are out of the loop, aren't you?" she smirks. "Ah, well, never mind. Sorry I bothered you. You're excused." She dismisses me with a wave.

Does she catch the bird I throw her way, through the vanity mirror? Of course not. She's too busy admiring her perfect profile, thanks to the best plastic surgeons money can buy.

Well, at least the next time I see Robert, I can put his mind at ease as to who's at the other end of the phone.

Lee is standing at the bottom of the stairs. He wags a finger at me. "Catherine has been waiting at least ten minutes."

"Hello to you, too," I say sweetly. "Sometime into the second hour, I got bored of waiting for her highness, so I thought I'd look up the lady of the house and pay my respects."

"Very kind of you." He frowns. "She's feeling neglected these days."

"I've got an inkling as to what might remedy that."

"A shopping spree?"

"You know your wife like a book."

"And from what I hear, you know the Martins almost as well."

I shrug. "People change with time."

He nods toward the library. "I think that's what Catherine is looking to hear from you. Why don't you assuage our candidate's worst fears?"

I nod, and head for the door.

The only one who can do that for her is Robert.

Something tells me she already knows this.

"WHY DID YOU DO IT?" CATHERINE KNOWS I'M HERE, BUT SHE doesn't even turn around.

"My mother's recipe may have gotten you a blue ribbon at the county fair, and the Tip Top Teen USA title, and a scholarship, but it will not get you the presidency of the United States."

She whips around. "You made me a national laughingstock."

"You're a mature adult; you'll get over it. I was a kid. It took a little longer."

"Ah, so you admit it! You're still holding a grudge because Robert was in love with me, not you."

"You're nuts! I had a schoolgirl crush, that's all."

"Then why did you drive off with him today?"

"He and Evan asked for a lift. What was I supposed to do, say no?"

She starts to speak, but changes her mind. Instead she proffers a limp hand and a mirthless smile. "Bravo. You've moved on. If you're truthful about that, I'll keep you on—for old times' sake."

I bite my tongue before I say something I'll regret, like *don't do me any favors*, or *kiss my ass*, or *he's leaving you ha ha booyah and there's nothing you can do about it.*

Instead, I remember the most important lesson my mother taught me:

I am a lady, at all times.

Had Mother known what Catherine did to us, I'm sure she would have approved of a quick kick to the gut. I guess I'll never know.

As I walk out the door, the dim buzz of a cell can be heard. Catherine blushes; then, with a nod of her head, I'm dismissed.

Through a mirror hung over a Louis XIV bombe chest, I watch as she reaches into her pocket and pulls out a hot pink cell phone. "Yes I can talk," she mutters.

Heck, if Lee wanted to reach her, why didn't he just knock and come in?

I have my answer when I reach the front door. He's standing right there, conferring with Lydia about all the calls that needed to be made by Catherine while she was scolding me.

Or talking to whomever.

Maybe Robert is right after all.

MARY KNOCKS ON MY BEDROOM DOOR AND WAITS FOR ME TO beckon her with a hand slathered with my night cream.

She holds something behind her back, and she's been crying.

Before I can say a word, she crawls into my lap for a hug.

As I pat her gently with the dry hand, I ask, "Honey, what's wrong?"

"I'm so sorry, Mom," she sniffles. "I hadn't realized that CeeCee was such a bitch!"

"CeeCee? You mean, Congresswoman—"

"I read your diary." She looks down at her feet. "Forgive me, please! I know it's an invasion of your privacy, but when I moved the box Aunt Phyllis left on the window seat to the floor, it toppled over, and the diary fell out. I thought it was cute, and I didn't think you'd mind, so I opened it."

Mary must be talking about the diary my mother gave me for my eleventh birthday. Mother had hoped I'd record all our wonderful mother-daughter adventures. Instead, I wrote about heartache, shame and death.

The poems seething of anger came later.

For at least a year, Bobby was on every page.

The squeeze of her hand reminds me that there are still more adventures to come: with her if not with Mother. And with Jack instead of Bobby. "You loved him, didn't you— Bobby, I mean?"

It takes me awhile to admit it, with a nod. "Yes—that is, I thought so, at the time." I shrug. "He was older, and he was kind to me. And your grandmother was dying, so thinking about him took me to another place that was certainly more enjoyable."

Mary leans her head on my chest. "CeeCee was so mean to you—and so jealous!"

"She was afraid of losing him. He was her world. When people are scared, they need someone to blame. They create monsters."

"Like Erin, with Babs," she murmurs. "I can't stand by and let them hurt her anymore."

"I know she'd be there for you, if the shoe were on the other foot."

She rises and heads for the door. "Mom, will you drive us to school tomorrow—all of us, Babs, too?"

"Of course."

"And would you mind if Babs and Wendy come home with me tomorrow?"

"Not at all."

"Great! That way, they'll meet Evan before he leaves—"

"What? No, Evan will be with his mother and father at Disneyland."

"Not after what I read him just now, in your diary!"

"Mary—you didn't! ... Did you?"

"Mom, he's already got his mother pegged, believe me. Sadly, it didn't surprise him."

Poor Evan.

Poor me.

13

Photo-Op

Short for "photo opportunity," an event staged specifically for news cameras to help a politician appear on the evening news or in morning papers. Usually, they say the exact same phrases, with the same inflections in their voices, with a smile on their faces.

They do this because they figure if you hear their malarkey enough times, you'll actually believe it. What they don't realize is that when you have children, every tall tale in the book has already been told to you, with even more practiced innocence than any number of photo ops will allow. So the next time you read or hear about a political photo op, do what you do when your kids come to you with a whopper:

Tune out, turn off, and tell off.

Your family will be saying "cheese" with big smiles when they bite into this:

Cheesy Hash (Recipe from Sheila L. Du Brutz, Harrah, Oklahoma)

Ingredients

- 1 package of frozen hash brown southern style square potatoes
- 1/2 cup of butter
- 1 pint of sour cream
- 2 cups of cheese

Directions

1. Melt butter in big pot, add sour cream, potatoes and cheese. Mix thoroughly.
2. Put in baking dish in oven at 375 degrees for 45 minutes.
3. Add more cheese to top it before serving, if you like.

Catherine has made it very clear to Ryan that I'm not supposed to broach the apple pie recipe again with her, under any circumstances.

And apparently she's livid that I had the nerve to mention it to, quote, that daughter of mine—who, in turn, has now turned her son against her, unquote.

Apparently Evan has asked her to 'fess up and apologize

to *me*. Of course, she refuses. She says it's my word against hers "that any of that malarkey even happened."

He says he'll settle for her allowing Mary to be his guest at Disneyland.

She's agreed to this option. I guess the only thing saving him from being banished from the campaign trail is that Catherine is more afraid of what her teenager will say or do when he's off her radar.

Join the club.

So that she has at least one adoring child at her side while the cameras are clicking away, she's invited Janie, Lee and Babette to join her. However, it annoys her that Janie is joined at the hip with Trisha. Then again, she must figure that having two children under the age of ten in the photo op burnishes her image as a youthful candidate who is concerned with children's issues because she finally breaks down and says yes to Janie's request.

It helps that Janie can hold her breath for a very long time, and that Catherine would rather not muss her lipstick giving the stubborn little girl mouth-to-mouth resuscitation.

At least on some level she has met her match.

With a shrug, Ryan adds, "Donna, you're on ghost surveillance. In fact, feel free to take the rest of your brood along—as cover, of course."

That's Ryan's way of warning me to keep out of Congresswoman Martin's sight.

"For additional reconnaissance, Emma and Arnie will be in the park, too," Ryan continues. "They can pretend to be a young couple in love, or something."

If only he knew how easy that role comes to them.

"And of course, Abu will be there, too," Ryan adds.

Abu's nod is nonchalant.

"I've got a friend at Disney Security who owes me a favor or two," Ryan says. "He'll let me into their webcam control room so I can direct his security team. After the attempt made on Governor Davis, make sure Congresswoman Martin wears a GPS tracker and surveillance contacts, so that we can see everything in her sight line. We can never let her go black."

He can say that again. We've been told that they anticipate 80,000 attendees at the park tonight.

It looks like the family Stone will be among them.

AT FIRST, JEFF'S FACE FALLS WHEN I TELL HIM WE'RE GOING TO Disneyland, but that he can bring just one friend. But then he starts building his case for why both Morton and Cheever should accompany us.

He rightly pointed out that if his administration is going to run smoothly, there needs to be a détente among him and Cheever. "I've extended the olive branch," is how he puts it. "This Cold War has gone on long enough."

"'Long enough?'" Yes, I am snickering. "The election was only a week ago!"

He shrugs. "First rule of politics—keep your friends close, and your enemies closer."

"Really? I thought the first rule was 'you can't win unless you're on the ballot.'"

"It depends on whom you're quoting," he counters. "I prefer Shakespeare over Rumsfeld."

He's got a point. And besides, with all the honing he's done on his debating skills, I'll admit it: I'm no match for him. "Okay, yeah, both the little hellions can come—but only because I'm extending my own olive branch to Mrs. Bing. It's what you call, 'tit for tat.'"

"Did you hear that? Your mom said 'titty!'" Morton elbows Jeff.

Jeff shoves back. "No, she said *tit*."

Morton pushes him again. "Same thing. Titty, tit, titty, tit—"

Jack smacks his head gently. "Where are your manners? There are ladies present."

The boys snicker. Still, in Jack's presence they're smart enough to keep their dirty little thoughts to themselves.

Lydia, Catherine's press secretary, has told the press corps that "Catherine is taking a personal day, just her and her close friends, the Chiffrays. She loves their children as if they were her own—"

What the …

Jack puts his hand over my mouth before I can yell out, "Trisha is not a Chiffray! She is a Stone!"

I can take a hint. Keep my eye on the prize: saving Catherine's ass, which means keeping my job.

Maybe it's time to retire.

In Congresswoman Catherine Connelly Martin's world, she is the sun, warming everything around her with her smile; creating an environment in which all others will certainly live long and prosper. Listening to the cheers, claps, shouts and murmurs of admiration that greet her as she ambles down Disneyland's Main Street with Lee, Babette, Janie and my daughter at her side, you'd think the public had bought into The World According to Catherine.

We—that is, the Acme security detail who orbit her—see things differently. The hot white glare of Catherine's political shenanigans cast too many troubling shadows, where the many enraged by them can hide—with a semi-automatic and a box of bullets. Until they reveal themselves, we are all in the congresswoman's gravitational pull, albeit not in orderly trajectories. Instead, we take turns orbiting her. Otherwise, we ebb and flow through the crowd, assessing everyone for their ability to do her harm.

"There are over a hundred thousand people here today, so stay on your toes," Ryan warns us from webcam central in Disney's security headquarters. "Our young lovers, Emma and Arnie, are lined up behind Snow White at the Alice in Wonderland ride. They should be out in another six minutes. Abu, you're next up at bat when they come out of there."

Abu murmurs, "Right, boss," into our ear buds.

Ryan is right about one thing—the kids are the perfect cover for Jack and me.

Maybe too perfect, considering how well they do their roles of driving us to distraction. "Stay, as a group, and always within sight! No pairing off!" That's my way of warning Mary that this family outing to Disneyland isn't going to turn into a three-hour game of hide-and-seek, just because Evan insists on hiding in plain sight of the reporters by tagging along with us.

But of course, they'll figure out how to ditch us. I just have to accept that.

And Evan will have to accept the fact that if I catch him rounding any bases, he'll be zapped with my taser gun, his mother be damned. In my mind, she's already a she-devil.

Jack warns, "Jeff, your mother's rule goes double for you and the Two Stooges."

Mary gives me a kiss. It is her way of reminding me that she's ready to earn my trust.

Jeff and his friends feel differently. They skedaddle before Jack can say another word.

Jack rolls his eyes. "The last thing we need is to lose Cheever."

I smile. "Don't worry. I put a GPS tracker on Jeff."

"You don't say. Unfortunately, if he and Morton ditch the little toady, we'd never hear the end of it from Penelope."

"Tell me about it. And I know just how she'd ask me to make it up to her, too." I reach up to give him a peck on the lips and wave *buh-bye*.

He frowns. "Are you insinuating I'd be her consolation prize?"

"She'd insist on it! You know she drools every time you come into view. I'm tempted to throw a bucket of water over her, just to cool her down."

He laughs. "Better not. She'd probably melt."

If only this truly was a fun-filled outing for the Family Stone. Instead, it's a work day for our Acme team. The way Catherine—code name, Snow White—is pumping the flesh ensures us of this.

"She rode a caterpillar with Janie and Trisha," Emma reports back. "There was no interaction with anyone else."

"She's leaving Space Mountain now," Abu responds. "Again, a lot of glad-handing, but no suspicious interference."

"The hitter is being cautious—making sure that she isn't being followed," Jack murmurs. "Ah, here she is now, a few feet from Donna and me. Everyone, take your places."

We hear a chorus of *Roger* in our ear buds.

I scan the crowd. Finally I spot Catherine's red-white-and-blue sunhat. She ushers the girls toward the Hyperion Theater, for the Aladdin show.

Jack stays a few steps behind the congresswoman. Always smiling for the cameras, she holds out one hand to Janie, and the other to Trisha. Seeing Jack, Trisha frowns and shakes her head, but Babette shoves her in Catherine's direction anyway.

I'd love to shove Babette into an alligator-infested moat. Too bad we aren't in front of Sleeping Beauty's Castle.

I queue up behind them. There are eleven or so people between us.

It takes fifteen minutes for the line to move into the auditorium. So that the cameras find her easily, Catherine makes sure to take a seat on the end of an aisle, just five rows from the stage.

Jack is lucky enough to end up in the same row, beside Trisha.

I rush to grab the seats in the row immediately behind Catherine.

Like all the other children in the theater, Trisha and Janie squeal excitedly as the lights dim and the show starts. But Jack and I are watching Catherine, not the show. The program claims it will run about seventy-five minutes. In the first ten minutes, we've already heard two fast-paced songs, and we've been awed by three colorful sets and the mood-setting lights, along with the smoke, scrims and mirrors that conjure up the story's mystical setting.

Suddenly I notice something is different about Catherine.

She's taller.

How could that be?

Because whoever is sitting there isn't Catherine.

Same hat, same outfit. But I'm not looking at Catherine's profile.

I crane my neck to look up the aisle. I see her—but she's no longer wearing a hat, and she is following the show's main character—the blue Genie—toward a side exit.

I say into my mic, "Jack—she's walking up the aisle, with the Genie!"

He looks around and sees what I see. "Follow them," he says. "I'll stay with the girls."

"And I'll send ops to pick up the imposter, and to back you up," Ryan murmurs into my ear.

By the time I reach the theater's reception area, they are nowhere to be found. Frantically I open a side door—

Just in time to see them disappear down a hallway, and around a corner. I run after them, but when I turn the corner, too, I find myself in yet another long corridor, with several doors on both sides. Each is marked with the name of a character in the show.

I open the first door labeled JASMINE. The room is empty.

Same for the second, third, and fourth.

When I open the fifth door, I see them—the Genie is holding a knife to her throat. She pulls away, frightened. He leers, pleased he has scared her into submission, and then steers her through another door with him.

Ryan's voice comes in through my ear bud. "Donna, chase him down! I'm sending Abu and Arnie as back-up!"

I bolt through the door, only to find myself in a very dark void. But I can see a light at the end of this very long tunnel, and I run toward it—

Oh my God, we're in back of the stage.

The audience is laughing and applauding wildly. Princess Jasmine and Aladdin have just finished a duet.

It's time for the Genie to go on.

Only there are two of them.

But only one is holding Catherine's hand.

Gotcha.

Just as the curtain parts, I let loose with a front kick, which takes him by surprise. He stumbles back, dazed, but recovers quickly, yanking the curved sword out of the hand of the real genie, who looks on in shock as his doppelganger swings it at my neck.

Granted I could use a haircut, but nothing so short that I'll lose my head over it, so I duck just in time. The sword whistles over my head.

My response takes him off balance.

This gives me the few precious seconds I need in order to jab him in the kidney. But he rights himself and comes at me again, swinging that damn sword. Quickly I duck and roll. While doing so, I grab the magic carpet off the floor and toss it over his head.

Blinded, he flails around the stage. I give him one big shove—

Which sends him into the orchestra pit.

The sword falls too, landing upright in his midsection. He cries out in pain.

I look up. The audience is dead silent.

Dead being the operative word here—

Until I hear my Trisha scream out, "Mommy! You killed Aladdin's Genie!"

I guess I have a lot of explaining to do.

I look over at Catherine for support. But no, she's frowning at me, her arms crossed at her waist. "You silly fool," she hisses. "You ruined a national photo op! I was to have some lines with the Genie! It was all part of the show!"

"But I thought … I saw him threaten you!"

Suddenly I'm surrounded by Disney security guards. They jerk my hands behind my back and hustle me off the stage.

I'm now branded the meanest Disney villain of all time.

The other actor also playing the Genie saves the day. He jumps out of a puff of smoke and belts out a happy pappy ditty, willing the eyes of all the little terrorized tots back onto the stage.

As the guards and I pass my family's seats, I hear Jack say, "See that, Trisha? Mommy didn't hurt the good Genie. She just saved Jasmine, Aladdin, and Congresswoman Martin from the bad one."

Is my daughter buying this bit of malarkey? From what I can hear, her sobs have lessened, but I may still be in for a scolding.

Or we'll both be in for years of therapy.

14

Political Suicide

A vote or action that is likely to be so unpopular with voters, as to cause a politician's probable loss in the next election—

Sort of like what you face when you promise your children you'll make brownies if they straighten up their rooms, but then you change your mind because you're on a diet, and you don't need a pan of bliss staring you in the face whenever you pass it. Next time, don't expect them to rush to do your bidding—or for that matter, leave you any crumbs.

Of course, to win back their hearts and minds, you can tempt them with a new sweet confection, like this one:

Death By Blizzard (From Carleen Nicholson, Dover, New Hampshire)

1. In a large Truffle bowl, layer the following:
2. Vanilla ice cream, about 2 inches thick.

3. Vanilla or tapioca pudding, about 2 inches thick
4. White chocolate morsels, a single layer
5. Cool Whip, about 2 inches thick. (Keep Cool Whip in freezer until just before use, it needs to be very firm to support the next layer)
6. Top this with scoops of vanilla ice cream around the edge.
7. In the center of this put another layer of white chocolate chip morsels.
8. Drizzle morsels with caramel sauce.
9. If you want to add a bit of crunch to it, add a layer of crushed ladyfingers just above the pudding layer.
10. Keep refrigerated until served.

"I know you hate the woman, but it's your job to protect her, so get out of bed." Jack yanks off the sheet from my mattress, exposing me as the fool I really am.

In a flannel granny gown, no less.

And yes, I'm hugging Trisha's teddy bear to my chest. He better not take that, too, or he's a dead man.

I grab for the sheet, but he holds it just out of reach.

I shrug as I mutter, "Go away! I almost killed a Disney character, in front of my young, very impressionable daughter."

"Donna, quit being so melodramatic. For goodness sake,

the darn sword is made of plasterboard. If and when he gets out of the hospital, he can rejoin the cast as the palace eunuch." He flips up the back of my granny gown to admire the view.

"How was I supposed to know Catherine's PR flack arranged for her to take the stage?" I yank it out of his hand and pull it back down, this time below my knees. "I'm off this assignment, remember? Catherine made it quite clear to Ryan that I'm to stay out of her sight for the rest of my life, or else risk being sent to Gitmo as a terrorist. The nerve of her! And by the way, if she's elected president, we're all moving to Canada. No, make that New Zealand, since it's not on her list of countries to invade, lucky Kiwis! But if an oil gusher pops up somewhere near Auckland, all bets are off on that country, too. We'll just have to find a deserted island to live on."

"Honey, please—quit feeling sorry for yourself." Jack pulls me up into his arms. "Don't you see? The fact that she doesn't want you around works in our favor. You can shadow her detail. Hide in plain sight."

"Frankly, if someone popped her, I could care less."

Jack's smile fades. "No arguments there. Catherine Martin is a conniving, devious bitch. She doesn't think about anything or anyone but herself. Her whole purpose in running for the presidency is to prove just how far she can go on Robert's money and goodwill." He raises my hand to his lips, and kisses it. "But Donna, she can't prove anything to you, because you already have her number. So tell me: if you save her life, don't you have the upper hand then? Hell, if she gets elected, at the very least she'd owe you a Congressional Medal of Honor."

He's got a point. Of course, she'd probably choke me with the medallion's sash when hanging it around my neck.

I nod grudgingly. "Okay, Genius. Let's say I agree to play shadow. How exactly do you see this scheme of yours working? After the Disney fiasco, Ryan has put me on permanent leave, remember?"

Jack shrugs. "What Ryan won't know won't hurt him. You may be the only thing standing between her and whatever bullet comes her way."

I sigh. "Okay, sure. I'll do what I can to take down her shooter—but only because I like the idea of her owing me her life."

He kisses my forehead. "Great, now get dressed. Four hours from now she's receiving the Zero Hunger America Humanitarian Award, at the Dolby Ballroom."

"Impressive. If only the voters knew she's leading the charge to gut the food stamp program by forty billion dollars over the next ten years." I shake my head in dismay. "Another two million people were tossed off the rolls with the last cut."

"You can express your personal distaste for her at the ballot box—if she lives that long." He tosses me an invitation to the event. It's black tie, of course.

"Nothing can kill her. The woman is like a cockroach." I head toward my closet. *Hmmm,* what does one wear to take down the killer of your worst enemy?

I pull out a dress I've been saving for just the right occasion: a floor-length chantel-beaded evening gown with a scoop neck and low back.

It is white. Should she prove me wrong, I don't plan on mourning her.

EVEN AT A THOUSAND DOLLARS A SEAT, THE HOLLYWOOD & Highland Center's cavernous Dolby Ballroom is packed solid with hobnobbers, do-gooders, up-and-comers, the glitterati, and political patrons of all stripes. With all of Catherine's competition demolished, the smell of victory is in the air, along with that of smoked flat iron steak with grilled peppers, and California olive-orange marinated Pacific sea bass topped with a caramelized mint fennel.

Because I'm incognito, I've accessorized the gown with a straight blond wig cut with bangs and an ear-length blunt razor cut, ice blue contacts, and a diamond choker and long white opera gloves. I've slipped into the ballroom just as the dinner portion of the event is ending. Much of the crowd is out of their seats, milling around. The line to pay homage to Catherine is at least thirty people long.

Robert is seated next to Catherine, in the front middle table with the director of Zero Hunger America, Beverly Kinkaid. I wouldn't doubt it in the least if Catherine had Robert strong-arm Beverly for the award, what with it being her year to run.

As her West Coast hosts, Babette and Lee are also part of Catherine's entourage. And at Catherine's behest, Jack is her official bodyguard, while Abu and Dominic are shadowing them. Abu is seated at a neighboring table, while Dominic pretends to chat up a socialite. Really, his eyes dart around the room, looking for anything suspicious.

Even from my table in the back, I'll see what Jack and Abu do, thanks to my video-linked contact lenses. The Acme team—which means by default, I, too—can hear Catherine's instructions to Jack, and his to us. While he calls the rest of the team out by name, he never utters mine—not even when Catherine baits him by murmuring, "I'm sure Donna would have enjoyed this. If only she had behaved herself!"

I have to give Jack credit. He doesn't even wince at her cattiness. On the other hand Abu mutters through a cough, "Bitch."

My sentiments exactly. But to keep my mind off of killing her myself, I focus on saving her life.

Only Catherine's security team is allowed to carry weapons into the Hollywood & Highland Center. All bags have been checked, no matter how chic, tiny or elegant. Arnie, who has been working in the cloakroom before covering the crowd as a waiter, slipped me my favorite Walther PPS when I handed him my white mink stole. Just six inches long and a shade over nineteen ounces in weight, it fits nicely in my clutch purse.

The ballroom is over twenty-five thousand square feet in size—broad, deep, and with towering ceilings. If a shooter is in fact here, he or she would have to be positioned within 2,700 yards of the stage, where Catherine will be receiving her award.

I scan the tables within shooting range. They are filled with celebrities, the wealthy, and the otherwise renowned. But unlike the theatre next door which hosts the Academy Awards, this room is not tiered with view boxes, and there is no balcony.

High above our heads, spot and track lights are affixed in strategic locations on the ceiling. For shows this size, there must be a tech control booth for lights and audio, and it has to be located in view of the stage …

Ah, there it is, high on the wall to the right-hand side of the stage is a large glass window. The room behind it is dark—

Wait … Did something just move up there?

Despite the fact that the ballroom lights are flickering to let the crowd know the speeches will start any moment now, I wind my way through the milling crowd, toward the back of the room. "Arnie, how would I access the stage tech room?" I whisper.

"Go back out into the lobby. Facing the ballroom, you'll see a door to the right of the ballroom. It's the staircase to the tech room."

"I'm on it. Abu, Dominic, I may need back-up. Jack, do what you can to cover Snow White."

"Will do," he murmurs back, "Watch your step."

That goes without saying when you're trying to take down an assassin in four-inch Loubies.

THE STAIRWELL CLIMBS UP TO A SECOND STORY. IT OPENS INTO A hallway that elbows around the ballroom's right side.

The corridor is so dark that at first I don't see the large lump of humanity in the middle of the hall—the body of a man, who was obviously shot trying to escape.

My guess is that the poor guy was hired to run the lights. Now someone else is opting for fireworks, when the time is right.

The door to the tech room is opened a mere crack.

I hold my gun low with both hands. I move forward slowly, hugging the wall until I reach the doorway. I listen for sounds, but all I hear is Beverly Kinkaid's voice.

She is telling touching tales about the Martins.

I crack open the door, just a few inches. This allows me to peek inside the room, which is dark, except for the light emanating from the stage two stories below. I can also see the barrel of an M110 semi-automatic sniper rifle. It is positioned in its bipod, which sits on a high table placed up against the window, which has a sliding panel.

No surprise, it is aimed at the podium.

So that I can see the shooter, I nudge the door open a few inches more—

Where the hell is he?

I get my answer when the door smacks my shoulder—so hard that I drop my gun.

My assailant yanks me into the room and slams my back up against the wall. Before I have time to react, he grabs my wrists with one hand, and cuffs them with plastic locking restraints with another.

When I shout, he slaps me across the face with the back of his hand. "No one can hear you." His growl is barely a whisper. "This booth is soundproof, so shut up already."

I realize he's right. It is through speakers that we hear the crowd laugh as Robert regales them with the often-told story of his infatuation with his childhood sweetheart, how everything he did in life was to garner her attention and earn her respect.

And, finally, her hand in marriage.

How, with her support, he built a multi-million-dollar business.

And how, with his support, she has followed her own dream, as he puts it: "to enrich the lives of others, through her unwavering commitment to public service."

Their eyes mirror his adoration for the woman who strives only so others may live their dreams.

Little do they know their worst nightmare is about to take place.

Mine already has.

Like every other man here, the shooter is dressed in a tux, except his face is hidden under a ski mask, and his hands are covered by latex gloves.

He pulls my hair back, revealing my Acme ear bud. He yanks it out and crushes it underfoot. I've gone dark to my mission team.

Why aren't they here by now?

He shoves me down into the chair in front of the rifle. As if reading my mind, he mutters, "The door from the lobby was set to auto-lock, just a minute ago." His voice is tinny. It's obvious he's talking through a microphone using voice changer software. "You got in by the hair of your chinny chin chin."

Lucky me.

And by the way, I don't have hair on my chin. Implying that I need electrolysis gives me reason enough to kill this son of a bitch.

As Robert and Catherine join Beverly at the podium, the shooter curls my hands on the grip. "You're just in time to pull the trigger." His nonchalant whisper sends a shiver up my spine. "What should we aim for? Head? Chest?"

I answer him with a head butt.

He groans and instinctively reaches up to touch his bruised cheek. I grab the rifle and leap up out of the chair. But as I whip around to take him out, he sidekicks me in the gut.

When I double over, he jerks the gun from my hand and tosses it on the table. Then he drags me by the handcuffs toward a steel storage closet door.

He tries the knob, but it's locked. "Too bad," he whispers hoarsely. "But this will hold you anyway." In no time, he's twisted one my wrists around the knob. He pulls duct tape from a duffle bag by the table, tears off a piece, and slaps it over my mouth.

No matter how hard I try, I can't pull away.

Applause floats up from the ballroom below us. As he slides open the window a mere inch, I push and strain to break loose from the knob, but I can't. I'm too far away to stop him, but I watch as he mounts the gun again, positions it through the window opening, and focuses the sight on his target.

From over his shoulder, I too can see the stage. Catherine feigns modesty by placing one hand demurely on her clavicle while she waves at the adoring crowd with the other. Any moment now, they will take a step back, so that she has the podium by herself. When that happens, her assassin will have his money shot, and there will be nothing I can do to stop him.

Nodding at Beverly and Robert, she seals her fate.

The crowd finally grows silent. I know she is talking, because I can hear her. Despite the warmth of her tone and the stridency of her speech, her words never register. Instead, they flutter around my brain. Her voice triggers memories of the CeeCee of my youth.

All the pinky swears we shared. All the broken promises she made.

All the heartache I experienced because of it.

All of my silly, unfounded hatred.

I was my mother's favorite. I've known this, all my life, despite trying to convince myself otherwise. She was sick and drugged when she called CeeCee by my name.

In answering her back, perhaps CeeCee granted her a kindness.

It's time I admit to myself what I really hated was that I felt guilty that I wasn't at my mother's bedside that afternoon.

I was with Bobby.

Because of the silencer on the assassin's rifle, no one hears the shot.

It takes a moment for the blood to appear.

Soon, screams echo through the hall.

Finally the body stumbles and falls—

Robert's body, not Catherine's.

I'm just as stunned as everyone else.

I freeze, but not the assassin. He leaves everything— leaves me—and walks out the door.

I'm sure he knows the fire door will give him safe passage out of the building. He'll strip himself of his ski mask first, and tuck it in under his jacket. As soon as he's opened the exit door and noted that the coast is clear, his latex gloves will go into his pocket.

He'll whistle as he goes down the street, as if he doesn't have a care in the world.

I know all this, because it's exactly how I would have handled this hit.

The building's security team will figure out soon enough where the shot came from. I should be readying myself for the questions, the accusations, the tears and the shame that comes with failing at your job.

But I'm not. Instead, I'm thinking of Bobby and the one kiss we shared, oh so long ago.

May he rest in peace.

15

Bleeding Hearts

A term describing people whose hearts "bleed" with sympathy for the downtrodden. This description is used primarily to criticize liberals who favor government spending for social programs.

And for your information, you do not qualify for a bleeding heart if you (a) give a homeless person a dollar, then take it as a tax write-off; (b) spend your grandma's Social Security check on a "Sign Up with a Friend" gym membership; or (c) write the local police chief a letter protesting deplorable prison conditions, just because your boyfriend was coerced into "giving" his new John Lobb loafers to a fellow inmate, the one night he slept in the drunk tank.

Roasted Artichoke Hearts (from Darien Coleman, Raleigh, North Carolina)

Ingredients

- 3 (15-ounce) cans of artichoke hearts
- 4 garlic cloves, quartered
- 2 teaspoons extra virgin olive oil
- Salt and Pepper
- 1 tablespoon lemon juice

Directions

1. Preheat oven to 375 degrees Fahrenheit
2. Drain artichokes in a colander and rinse to remove brine
3. In a bowl, mix gently with garlic and olive oil.
4. Pour artichoke mixture into a metal roasting pan, and roast for about one hour, tossing a few times to roast evenly.
5. Sprinkle with lemon juice and salt and pepper, to taste.

THE FUNERAL IS TO BE HELD IN THEIR HOMETOWN OF Libertyville, Massachusetts, in the cemetery of the Pentecostal church where Catherine worships.

"It's going to be a three-ring circus," Jack predicts. "The media is split into two camps—those who feel she's too grief-stricken to go on with the campaign, and those who feel she's been catapulted into the presidency because of her loss."

"I hate to say it, but agree with the latter," I murmur.

"You and me both," he says. He holds me in his arms, as if he's afraid to let me go.

He was so worried that the assassin killed me first that he left Dominic with Catherine after the shooting, in order to join Abu and Arnie in finding me. The operations manager of the ballroom was so nervous that he forgot the code to open the auto-lock on the stairwell to the tech room, where the assassin set up. Thank goodness Arnie had a laser knife on him. Otherwise, I would have been up there all night. When Jack ran into the room, he bundled me up and got me out of there, fast.

Ryan called Jack on the carpet for leaving his post, but he is still so angry at me that I've yet to be called into the office. With my fingerprints on the rifle I'm sure I'll be hearing from someone soon. Better it be Ryan than the Feds with a one-way ticket to Gitmo.

Been there, done that.

Since the incident, Mary has been comforting Evan—lately, by phone, since he's flown home to Massachusetts with his mother and his father's body.

I find Mary sitting in the hammock in the back yard. Her cheeks are damp with tears.

"They're doing it in some Pentecostal church. Evan hates the thought of having it there!" she declares. "They only started going there three years ago, because the minister has a lot of clout. Evan says his father had faith, but didn't belong to any church. Mr. Martin wanted to be cremated and have his ashes scattered in the woods, behind their farm." She turns on her side, away from me. "Mom, I don't blame you for not liking

Congresswoman Martin, but we have to go to support Evan." She wiped away an errant tear. "I do, anyway. I'll take the ticket money from my allowance savings, if you prefer I go alone."

"Of course not. We are all going, as one family in support of another," I reassure her. "Mr. Martin was my friend, and so is Evan. And … well, I've made my peace with Congresswoman Martin."

I go upstairs to help my daughters pack.

Neither owns a black dress.

When we go out to buy one for each of them, nothing seems right.

I remember Robert complimenting their pink floral sundresses. I wish they could wear those instead, but as it is, I'm treading a very thin line when it comes to appropriate behavior.

After all, I am the one person who might have stopped his assassination.

No, pretty in pink just won't do.

THE WEATHER IN LIBERTYVILLE, MASSACHUSETTS IS ANYTHING but gloomy. Robert is being buried on a day that sparkles with a blanket of dew warmed by an early September's bright sun.

I may have forgiven Catherine, but now that we're here, it's obvious she hasn't done the same for me.

The funeral is attended by everyone who's anyone in

Washington. Catherine's staff and her party's leaders flank her on all sides, as if any one of them would take a bullet if it comes her way. The cemetery dates back to the eighteen-hundreds. It is lined with trees and a picket fence. Unfortunately, it's also close enough to the street that the army of reporters who have shown up can get the money shot they seek: the stoic widow in elegant Armani, her eyes red but dry, her head held high.

The Secret Service is here, too. Robert's death has put an end to all the public posturing of those candidates who are left in this race to do without, in order to save taxpayer dollars. Better they should save their own lives.

I'm sure they're all secretly relieved. I know their families are, too. None of the spouses signed on for anything more anxiety-ridden than state dinners, Easter Egg hunts on the White House lawn and a sex scandal or two.

The minister thunders through platitudes of a man he didn't really know before segueing into a sermon that lays the blame on "a world that is morally corrupt, and desperately needs strong and fearless leadership to guide it." The way he places his hand on Catherine's shoulder leaves no doubt as to where he feels the answer to his prayer lies.

And yes, all of this was caught on camera, and will be replayed ad infinitum on our twenty-four-hour news cycle.

After the coffin is lowered into the ground, the crowd surges around Catherine and Evan to offer their condolences. My family and I hang back until Evan motions us forward. His mother greets Jack and my children warmly, but despite my tears and my choked-up apology, she refuses to do more than nod curtly at me.

This unnerves Mary to no end. Her way of showing it is to ignore Catherine in kind. This is easy for her to do, since Evan seems to be doing the same.

Babette follows Catherine's lead and looks right through me. On the other hand, Lee pumps Jack's hand and kisses my cheek. He whistles when he sees the bruise on my cheek, then he whispers, "Sorry you got roughed up. Donna, what happened to Robert wasn't your fault. You did your best, but fate played a different hand."

I frown. "Sadly, it wasn't enough. Tell me, Lee—is Catherine dropping out?"

A shadow of a smile appears on his lips. "Are you kidding? She's going to win by a landslide."

"And who will be her running mate?"

Before he can answer, Babette calls him over. He makes his good-bye with a slight bow, then heads over to Babette and Catherine, who are already making their way toward their waiting limo.

Evan insists on riding with us back to the farm, where a reception is being held, this time for family and friends only.

I HAVE COME HERE TODAY, TO DO JUST ONE THING:

Apologize.

It's harder to do than you think, and not because I tear up at the memory of my mother or at the shame I have because

I couldn't stop the assassin who took Robert's life. The truth is that I can't seem to get Catherine alone. From POTUS on down, it seems that, like me, everyone feels the need to have a personal word with the grieving widow.

Before I give up on this very personal mission, I've decided to wait it out in the Martins' beautiful box hedge garden, just outside the rambling farm home's library. I'm only out there a mere ten minutes when I hear Catherine's voice, on the other side of the open library's French doors.

I turn around to see her pacing back and forth. Her body is rigid, like a rock holding its own against a menacing cyclone.

The cell phone she holds in her hand is hot pink.

It was the mysterious phone that concerned Robert to no end. If the person on the other end of the phone is a lover, what is he saying to make her so upset, on this day of all days?

Just then she turns toward the window. I whip around in another direction, shielding my eyes with one hand while feigning interest in a plane flying overhead.

A few moments later, I hear, "Yoo hoo! Donna! So glad I could catch you before you left," Catherine says, as she walks my way. Her mouth is set in a thin, firm line.

I hope my wave puts her at ease. "Oh … I'm so glad you found me here. You were busy with so many others that I thought it best to wait until the crowd thinned a bit to pay my respects."

Her relief that I don't acknowledge the scene I just saw in the window is evident in her eyes. She sits down beside me on the bench. "We're old friends, Donna. The fact that you and your family came all this way to support me—and Evan, of course—means a lot to me." Her brittle smirk proves otherwise.

Still, I'm ready to take her at her word. "Catherine, I want to say I'm sorry."

Her eyes lose all brightness. "You want me to forgive you for Robert's death." She states it as a fact, not a question.

"No ... I mean, I want to apologize for all the hate I've felt for you, all these years."

Her lips turn down at the edges. "Oh, really? Donna, admit it! You're still nursing the little girl crush you had on him!"

"No, of course not!" Jeez, can't the woman take an apology? Trust issues, anyone? "This has nothing to do with Bobby ... *Robert.* What I meant to say is that I hated you because of your relationship with my mother."

She tilts her head, intrigued. "I ... I don't remember—"

"You visited her, when she was sick, with cancer." The thought still chokes me up.

Her eyes are blank. Almost soulless.

She doesn't remember.

And I've never forgotten.

"Surely you remember. My father was out, and I had to go back to school to ... to get something."

A kiss. My very last one, from Bobby.

"In fact, just as I walked in, she called you ... by my name." My cheeks feel as if they're on fire.

She searches her memory. It comes to her with a snap of

her finger. "Ah, yes! That was somewhat embarrassing, to say the least."

I nod, relieved that she finally gets it. "Yes, exactly. I felt the same way."

She shrugs and looks up at the sky. A stray news heli-copter is still circling overhead. "I guessed her drugs were making her hallucinate. I mean, anyone in her right mind would have known better, right? You were such a pudgy little thing back then! And the way you wore your hair—it was always a mess!"

"I wouldn't exactly say I was pudgy."

"No, I guess you wouldn't. But Bobby did. He'd know, of course. Because you let him feel you up." Her eyes bored holes through me. "But your stomach roll *grossed him out.*" She bares her teeth into a smile. "He made a great decoy, didn't he? He didn't want to do it, but I begged him. I made him realize how important it was. He finally said yes." She swats the air, as if any memory of her scheme deserves a quick dismissal. "While he kept you busy, I asked your mother for her recipe, and she gave it to me."

"Only because she thought you were me." I turn to face her. "You did that on purpose, didn't you?"

"Perhaps." She shrugs. "Let's just call it a lucky accident —for me, anyway. You see, without it, I would have never won the county fair prize. And it served me well as my talent entry for Miss Tip Top Teen. From that, I got a scholar-ship to college—to Bobby's school, then on to Harvard Law. And the rest is history. So I guess I owe my political career to your mother." She pats my hand and rises. "Or Bobby, for being willing to do anything I asked of him. You see, I was always his one and only love." She mocks me with a sigh. "My Bobby was *such* a big strapping boy, a regular Adonis. But darling, lifelong love trumps first love every time. We both know that."

It would be so easy to punch her in the gut.

To crush her larynx with my fist.

To bury her under her well-pruned box hedge.

But I'm too much of a lady for that.

Instead, I get up and walk back into the house with my head held high.

Besides, I've already erased my mother's pie recipe from her computer, so that she can never use it again.

Jack sees me eyeing the door. Together, we gather up the kids, and we're out of there.

I try hard to hold my tears on the flight back to Orange County. But the moment we are home and the children are tucked in bed, I go to my own room and pull the blankets over my head.

Jack is there to kiss the tears away.

Catherine is right about one thing: Lifelong love trumps first love every time.

16

Convention

A national meeting of a political party, where delegates formally select a party's nominee. In most cases, they aren't casting their ballots based on who they may necessarily want to see as their party's candidate, but acting as sheep and reiterating the results of the party's chosen frontrunner—just like the primary voters in their respective states did before them.

However, every now and then, renegade delegates will summon the gumption to eschew the primary winner, and vote for the candidate they feel will do right by their vision of the party, as reiterated in the "platform"—or goals—of their favorite candidate.

However, in doing so, they can kiss their delegate status goodbye for the next convention, because it ain't a "party" if you make your host angry by snubbing the guest of honor: the presidential nominee with the most primary votes.

I'm sure that a lot of wonderful food is served at these

events (unless you're one of the protesters standing outside the police barricade—in which case, get used to prison food). Since I've never been to a delegate convention, I'll take this opportunity to use a little word play ("convection" as opposed to "convention") in order to demonstrate the joys of cooking with a convection oven, which circulates the heat within the oven, allowing your dishes to cook evenly on all sides:

Convection Oven Roasted Stuffed Turkey Tips (Molly Stevens, author, "All About Roasting")

These tips will help the turkey cook more evenly, brown more readily and give you plenty of crisp skin (and because it's stuffed).

- Set your temperature to a lower or moderate oven heat — no higher than 325 degrees convection, and consider 300 degrees convection if you have the time.
- To brown evenly, rub butter or oil on the skin before roasting.
- Your turkey should be done within three to four hours, depending on the size. The best way to know is to test it with an instant read thermometer, the stuffing should register 165 degrees.

Another hint on getting crisp skin: let the turkey sit

uncovered in the refrigerator for twenty-four hours before cooking.

THE DAY AFTER WE GET HOME, I GET THE SUMMONS I'VE BEEN waiting for, from Ryan.

Jack and I have just shut his office door behind us when he roars, "What the hell were you thinking?"

If his glass-walled office is indeed soundproof, why has everyone in the office turned their heads our way?

Granted, you could make a case that they are fixated by the way in which he is pacing the floor and tearing at what little hair he has left—until he realizes they are staring, and bangs on the glass with his fist as a warning that any one of them may be next on the cutting block.

That certainly sends them ducking back below their cubicle walls.

"It's my fault, Ryan," Jack insists. "I asked her to shadow us. Heaven knows we needed an extra set of eyes on this mission. And frankly, if she hadn't been there, we wouldn't know where to find the shooter."

Ryan's eyes slide from Jack to me. "That's just it. You missed your chance to take him down—and in doing so, you made things worse for yourself, Donna."

"But until last night, none of the candidates we covered were killed, let alone in any physical peril," I countered. "That's got to count for something!"

"My dear Mrs. Stone, have you noticed that each of their

campaigns imploded the moment you were sent in to cover them?" Ryan shakes his head in awe. "Let me congratulate you. With Robert Martin's death, you've officially earned the reputation of political cooler." He shrugs. "Trust me, his kill is a major stain on Acme's reputation as well. Now, neither party wants anything to do with us."

"Ryan, I get it. I screwed up royally, and an innocent man paid with his life. If you want to sideline me for a month or two—"

"I don't think you get the severity of the situation." Ryan leans in over his desk. "Depending on the DOJ investigation now in progress—not to mention any lawsuit the DNC wants to throw our way—you may be looking at permanent termination at the very least, if not an obstruction-of-justice indictment."

Jack slams his fist against the wall. "But Acme has a security contract!"

"Had, not has. As we speak, their lawyers are filing a breach-of-contract suit, on the basis that Donna was specifically asked to stay away, by the candidate herself. I'm sure there will be a major-damages suit to follow." Ryan shrugs. "And the fact that Donna's fingerprints are on the shooter's rifle is cause enough for a DOJ investigation."

"I'm sorry about that, Ryan—and not because I give a hoot what either the Dems or the GOP thinks of me, but because Robert was a very old and very dear acquaintance who … who happened to be in the wrong place, at the wrong time."

"Maybe. Maybe not," Jack mutters.

I turn to him. "I beg your pardon?"

Jack shrugs."Doesn't anyone else find it somewhat convenient that he should have died, just before the Democratic Convention? Have you seen how it's spiked her ratings in the polls?"

Ryan frowns. "But she had the damn nomination practically sewn up anyway."

"The nomination, yes. But not the election," Jack counters.

It's wishful thinking on his part.

I shake my head adamantly. "You're wrong, Jack. Robert was the love of her life."

He shrugs. "Yeah, I know. Childhood sweethearts, yada yada."

"It's much more than that. They've already been through so much together." I stop myself there. I shudder at the thought of reliving my last conversation with Catherine. "As much as I personally have never liked the woman, I think I know her well enough to say she'd never cross such a line."

Even in death, I feel the obligation to honor Robert's secrets and doubts about their marriage.

If that means saving Catherine's ass, then so be it.

Jack may want to argue the point, but I don't.

I walk out Acme's front door, wondering if I'll ever be invited back.

"CAN YOU BELIEVE IT? THE DELEGATES ARE FALLING OVER

themselves to vote for that woman!" Mary, who has been staring at the televised DNC convention proceedings, shakes her head in disgust.

"Well, of course she'd zip up the nomination," Jeff says through a mouthful of peanut butter and jelly. "The polls have shown the congresswoman spiking since the funeral. Even committed delegates have been changing their votes, they're so inspired by her strength under such adversity."

Mary throws a pillow at him. "My God, that's a verbatim soundbite CNN has been repeating all day!"

Jeff throws it back at her. "Can I help it if I've memorized it? Hell, it's all anyone says on the damn boob tube—"

"Jeff, if your mother hears you curse, you'll get a mouthful of soap," Jack warns him. "Enough already, both of you! Give it a break!"

They quiet down, but their eyes stay fixated on the TV screen, where the crowd of DNC delegates shouts above the band blaring *Happy Days Are Here Again*. Blue and white balloons tumble from the roof of the ballroom in a shower of glittering confetti as Catherine strides onto the stage, waving triumphantly to those who have just voted her their party's nominee to be the next president of the United States.

Even when the band stops playing, the crowd's roar only grows louder. Congresswoman Catherine Connelly Martin stands tall at the podium, in an elegant royal blue dress. Her eyes glisten triumphantly as she scans the room. She seems to glow as if she is absorbing their admiration into every cell of her body.

Finally her audience grows silent. When she speaks, her voice never wavers, but gets stronger with each sentence. She talks of adversity, and sacrifice, and family. She decries a world of hatred, fear, and terror, calling instead for one in which prosperity reaches "every city, every town, every village and every person." She warns the crowd that the tasks ahead won't be easy. "It will take each and every one of us to fight the war on hatred. To take down those whose aim is to oppress us—not just physically, but mentally, emotionally, fiscally, and morally."

"With that last line, she's thrown in every platitude there is," Jack murmurs.

Not quite. There's more to come. Next, she hones in on the real point of her speech—that "you, the American people, can never forget what has made us strong in desperate times. Well ladies and gentlemen, times are once again desperate! This is why I call on you, once again, to be strong! To, like me, use your tragedy as the catalyst to right the world—your world." She pauses. "Our world."

A picture of Catherine and her family, arm in arm, appears on the JumboTron screen behind her. A moment later, a faint halo glows behind Robert's head.

Catherine stares at the screen for a moment, then reaches up, as if to embrace it. "A man does not die for something which he himself does not believe in," she declares. She then turns back to face the crowd. "All great movements are popular movements. They are the volcanic eruptions of human passions and emotions, stirred into activity by ruthless tragedy, or by the torch of the spoken word cast into the midst of the people. May my husband's tragedy light the way for us all!"

"Seriously, did she just quote *Mein Kampf*?" Jeff taps away on his iPad, hoping to find a citation for the passage.

Jack shakes his head in awe. "I hope Hilldale Middle holds onto this Civics teacher."

Mary groans. "When did you turn into such a little nerd?"

Jeff's retort is lost as his sister shushes him and points toward the TV. "Listen! I think she just announced that Mr. Chiffray was going to be … *her running mate*?"

All eyes turn back to the TV set. Lee bounds onto the stage next to Catherine. They clasp their hands and raise them and bow to the crowd.

Jack lets loose with a long whistle. "I guess now we won't be the only ones trying to figure out the mysterious Mr. Chiffray."

"If they do, I hope they let his wife in on the secret. She's dying to know."

"I am so proud to have Lee by my side," Catherine declares. "He is a tech industry leader and visionary who has been welcomed in the homes and hearts of world leaders everywhere. As a person with no experience in Big Government—but decades of experience in big ideas that have paid off in big dividends for his stockholders—Lee will play an integral role in my mission to streamline our government, and to attract the best and the brightest. No more 'government as usual.' It's time to make your government accountable—to see it pay off—for you, our country's stockholders!"

Catherine takes a step back so that Lee can take a solo bow in the spotlight.

On cue, all the crowd placards flip to their back sides. No longer do they read WIN WITH MARTIN, but now say GOVERNMENT: PAY OFF!

Jack snorts so hard, he almost falls off the couch.

Mary smacks his arm. "Dad, please be quiet! Evan just walked on the stage! Oh my God, he looks so sad!"

Babette and Janie walk on stage, nudging Evan to accompany them. Catherine takes his arm in hers, as if she'll never let him go.

I guess that's why the kid looks so scared.

I can't take it anymore. I stumble into the kitchen, looking for anything to keep myself occupied, so that my mind doesn't ponder the obvious outcome playing out, right before our eyes:

Catherine may be our next president.

Alas, my suspension has made me manic in all my housewifery tasks. The dishes are done. The floor is swept. The windows sparkle like diamonds. The cake I made earlier this afternoon has been iced, and dinner is warming in the oven.

My eyes roam hungrily around the room for a minuscule task:

The box left by Aunt Phyllis now crammed under the window seat.

Next stop, the garbage can.

I pick it up and take it out the back door.

Our dogs won't take the message that I'm in no mood to play with them right now. I sidestep Rin Tin Tin, only to hear Lassie yelp when I step on her paw. I back up into the trash can when she jumps up onto me, and the box falls, scattering its contents all over the driveway.

This puts me on my hands and knees, gathering up the flotsam and jetsam of my so-called 'tween life. A Rubik's Cube. An *Alf* lunch box. A boom box. A Mary Lou Retton poster, and one of The Clash. And an avalanche of cassette tapes. As I toss them back into the box, the juke box in my brain skips from one tune to the next. First Michael Jackson mourns *Billy Jean*. Next, The Police contemplate *Every Breath She Takes*. In homage of Bobby's kiss, I almost cut my hair like Annie Lennox. Why not look like her? The words, *Sweet Dreams are Made of This*, expressed so perfectly my hope that he'd finally leave CeeCee for me.

What a fool I was back then.

Not much has changed.

The seam of a manila envelope has split open. Its contents litter the driveway. I bend down quickly, in order to pick them up before the breeze scatters them beyond my reach. They are mostly condolence cards, addressed to my father and me, and dated the week of my mother's funeral. Back then I was too distraught to read them, and left most of them, unopened, on my mother's kitchen counter.

Aunt Phyllis must have shoved them in the envelope for

safekeeping, where they stayed, the year I met and fell in love with Carl; even after my father's death.

My mother would have been shocked at the thought that I'd never acknowledged the condolences of those who reached out to my father and me. Out of shame, I do so now.

My eyes tear up as I read their written thoughts of the woman I thought I knew so well. They describe her as "funny and bright," and "always there for others" and "a friend indeed."

How I could use her now.

When I get to a card addressed solely to me, the handwriting stirs a long-lost memory. Inside is a letter as opposed to a card.

It is signed by Bobby, and dated the day before my mother died. I flip over the envelope. Yes, the postmark is the same date.

The letter reads:

Dear Donna,

I want to apologize for any pain I may have caused you. I know I must have hurt you pretty badly because you no longer look in my direction and you walk off whenever I'm around. What CeeCee did was mean. And I was stupid to let her talk me into leading you on. She said you were like some of those girls who will do anything for a guy, even if he's someone else's boyfriend. I didn't realize until it was too late that you aren't like that at all.

You probably hate me, and I don't blame you. But I still want you to know that I'm only with CeeCee because she's got no one else in her life (her parents suck) and she's not half as strong as you are.

She's not half as pretty, either.

If you ignore me from now on, I'll understand. Just do me a favor and don't let anyone take advantage of you like I almost did. You're too sweet. No guy deserves you.

Okay, maybe I do. At least I hope you'll think so one day and forgive me.

I'll look you up when you're a senior, when I'm home from college.

XXX and I mean it,

Bobby

This must be the snub Robert referred to, regarding that day so long ago after my high school's basketball game, a few years after our last kiss.

By then, the chasm in my heart had opened even deeper. Mother was gone, and Father was drinking himself to death.

I no longer need Bobby to warn me against boys like him. I'd found my solace on the firing range, with my Lady Smith & Wesson.

Still, it would have been nice to have him around, to share jokes and dreams and secrets.

To kiss again.

No doubt Catherine misses his kisses, too. No amount of votes will change that.

If she doesn't realize that already, she'll find out soon enough.

17

Witch Hunt

In politics, this is a vindictive, often irrational, investigation that preys on the public's fears of political candidates behaving badly.

It would be nice if they weren't so often proven right.

The reference originally refers to witch hunts that took place in 17th-century Salem, Massachusetts, where many innocent women accused of witchcraft were burned at the stake or drowned.

Another fairy tale has a witch handing Snow White an apple. Here's an updated, even more delicious recipe for this always tempting fruit:

Apple Dumplings (From Donna Rich, Cape Hatteras, North Carolina)

Ingredients

- 2 Granny Smith Apples – peeled, cored, and cut into eight wedges each.
- 1 can Grands-type buttermilk biscuits, separated
- 1 stick Butter
- 3/4 cup of Sugar
- 1 cup of Water
- 1 ½ tsp Cinnamon and ¼ tsp Sugar

Directions

1. Roll each biscuit flat.
2. Top with an apple wedge, and seal around the edges
3. Place in 9 x 13-inch baking dish.
4. Bring the stick of butter, water and sugar to a boil, to create a sauce.
5. Pour the sauce over biscuit wedges.
6. Sprinkle with cinnamon sugar mixture. (A dash of nutmeg may also be added.)
7. Bake at 350 degrees, for 30 minutes, or until browned and bubbly.
8. Let cool, then enjoy with ice cream or whipped cream!

A PERSONAL SUMMONS FROM RYAN TO COME TO ACME'S OFFICES as soon as possible has me floating on air.

Unfortunately, I get it during my volunteer time in the

Hilldale Middle School's lunch room. I'm supposed to be doling out Brussels sprouts, but the kids only want them as Milk Pong pucks, so when Hayley isn't watching, I whisper to the kids that I'm fronting a tournament with a ten-dollar prize for the winner.

In no time at all, I'm out of sprouts, and outta there.

When I walk into Acme, I do look marvelous. Five-inch heels and a body-hugging sweater over a pencil-thin skirt with a slit in the back that reveals the black seams crawling up my stockings will do that for a girl.

I'm dressed to remind Ryan why he's always considered me one of Acme's most valuable assets: because I'm a sexy femme fatale who, with a single finger—placed tantalizingly on his lips, or curled around a gun trigger—can get any man to divulge his deepest, darkest secret.

During my suspension period, I've been doing a little soul searching. My quest has turned me upside downward dog (yoga) and into the conjugation of verbs (French) and to the end of a six-mile run.

During my worst days, my search takes me to the bottom of a bottle of a highly rated Pinot Noir.

If today goes well, my journey is over. Like Dorothy and her little dog, Toto, I've clicked my heels and come home to my Kansas: this nondescript campus of glass office buildings, somewhere over the 405.

I spot Jack standing by Arnie's cubicle. When he sees me, his eyes open wide. I would have expected a welcoming smile. Instead, a frown tugs at his lips. His eyes shift toward Ryan's door, as if he's afraid my mere presence there will cause the world to implode. Little does he know, it has finally righted itself.

They love me! They really, really love me!

I'm dying to hear what mission Ryan has lined up for me—

Who's that in Ryan's office with him?

Oh … Hell. *Army Major Blake Reynolds.*

Well, at least he's alone. Whenever he comes looking for me, it's usually with a SEAL team unit because Carl left Reynolds with the impression that I'd helped him escape from Gitmo.

Okay, maybe the fact that Reynolds found me sunning (make that burning) myself on Musha Cay with 10 six-inch bricks of Euros strewn on the bed of my sumptuous villa led him to jump to the wrong conclusion. Go figure.

"Donna! So glad you could join us!" Ryan acts as if we're at a garden party, not another of Reynolds' Gestapo-worthy interrogations. "You remember Major Reynolds, don't you?"

"Forget the man who perp-walked me out my front door? Never," I mutter. "By the way, Major Reynolds, I'm sending you the bill for my ruined flower beds. Your SWAT team isn't very light in their loafers."

"They wear jack boots. It goes with the territory." He shrugs. "You have an uncanny ability of showing up in the most unusual places, Mrs. Stone. The latest example is a doozy. How is it that you ended up in the room where Presidential Candidate Martin's husband's assassin was hiding?"

"I've already explained that—several times, in fact. I was

the first one to get there before the assassin could take down his target."

"And your presence there was unsanctioned, too," he prods.

I feel myself blushing. "Yes, okay, I've already admitted to that. It's why I'm currently on suspension, remember?"

"If that's the case, you failed miserably."

"Tell me about it," I mutter. The sad look on Ryan's face makes me want to cry, but I hold back my tears. "You don't need to remind me. Robert Martin was an old and dear friend."

"Yes, that's what I've heard," Reynolds says solemnly. "And it certainly fits with the information given to us by the presidential candidate."

I look from him to Ryan and back again. "What exactly are you talking about?"

"Candidate Martin mentioned your relationship with the deceased—and with her, as well." He shakes his head, as if grieved. "She blames herself for allowing you on her security squad. She never dreamed that you'd still hold a grudge, more than twenty years later, because she stole your high school sweetheart."

"*My* high school sweetheart? Is that what CeeCee said? Bobby was her boyfriend, not mine!"

Reynolds can't hide his smirk. "Did that upset you?"

"Yes! … I mean, no! It was a silly little crush on an older boy. No more."

"So when you pulled the trigger, were you aiming at the

woman who stole the one you thought you loved, or at the guy who spurned you?"

"Are you crazy? You've been reading too many young adult novels, Blake. Better go back to your law journals, or porn mags, or whatever it is that titillates you. I've had enough of this malarkey." I head for the door.

"The investigative reports that land on my desk are intriguing enough for me. For example, your fingerprints are on the murder weapon, Mrs. Stone. Not only that, the security cam footage blows your claim to smithereens that an assassin was with you in the tech room, or that he may have slipped out of the Hollywood & Highland Center through a back exit door. In fact, the only person on camera going into the tech room is you."

I shake my head. "All that means is that he deleted any footage in which he appears." I think for a moment. "What about the security stream in the tech room itself?"

He shakes his head. "There wasn't any."

"Since every nook and cranny in the place is covered, don't you find that just a little bit odd?"

"Yeah, okay, I grant you that." He shrugs. "But when I weigh that little anomaly against the word of someone who has ongoing dealings with known terrorists—"

"You're bringing up Carl—again?" I shake my head in disbelief. "I took Carl out myself, Blake—unless there's something you know that I don't."

"Yeah, sure, whatever you say." He smirks. "Just like you insist that your feelings for Bobby Martin died long ago."

Realizing I can't hide the pain I feel whenever I hear

Bobby's name, I turn my head down. I am now looking down at my feet.

The seams of my stockings are crooked.

Story of my life.

"Right now, you're our lead suspect in an ongoing investigation," Reynolds informs me. "Despite Mr. Clancy's insistence on vouching for your motive for being there, I must warn you that any attempt to leave the country will be seen as an admission of guilt. You will be tracked down as a terrorist, and as a threat to national security. In the meantime, should you come within even a mile of Presidential Candidate Martin, her security detail has orders to shoot to kill."

I dismiss his concern with a wave. "No need to worry. I have no desire to see CeeCee Martin again, in my life. As for leaving the country, I'll be around as long as Robert's killer is still at large."

Someone has to track him down.

I look forward to proving Reynolds wrong, yet again.

18

Dark Horse

A little-known candidate who is considered a long-shot in winning an election is called a "dark horse." The term, which dates back as far as 1842, originated in the horseracing profession.

There may have been a few times in your life when you were the dark horse. For example, you may have thought you lost the adoring affections of some man to another, only to have him circle around again. Or you may have arrived late to your airline gate. But instead of giving your seat away, they upgraded you to first class.

In either case, you're the winner.

The lesson here: the race isn't over until it's over.

Another lesson: there are different recipes for horseradish. This one adds a tang, and a little color:

Dark Horseradish Recipe (From Alexa Tierney, Louisville, Kentucky)

Ingredients

- 1 cup peeled and cubed horseradish root
- 2 teaspoons white sugar
- 3/4 cup dark infused vinegar
- Salt to taste

Directions

1. In an electric food processor or blender, process horseradish root, vinegar, sugar and salt.
2. Carefully remove the cover of the processor or blender, keeping your face away from the container. Cover and store the horseradish in the refrigerator.

"How was your day, honey?" The tone of Jack's voice is even more effervescent than the splash of tonic in my now thrice nightly vodka tumbler.

He asks out of courtesy. We both know I am bored almost to tears.

While he's off making the world a safer place, I'm relegated to the role of just another housewife in the OC.

Yep, it's official. My services at Acme Industries are no longer required—

Thanks to November's landslide victory for the ticket of Martin and Chiffray.

Perhaps changing their slogan from "Government: Pay Off!" to "Government Secure and Successful" had something to do with it. More than likely, the voting public hasn't yet figured out that "secure" is short for "more spying on everyone" and that the word "successful" only describes those lucky enough to secure the government contracts to do the spying on the rest of us.

It's been two months since the election. While there has been no further word from Major Reynolds of any impending arrest, it's no secret that I, for one, am under constant surveillance. Anything can and will be used against me—albeit not necessarily in a court of law. Gitmo isn't co-ed yet, but Catherine will see to it that I'm the exception to that rule.

I'll admit it, orange does nothing for my complexion, so I plan on behaving myself. Maybe there's no better time than now to convince Jack to move the whole family to Paris. From what I hear, the French don't like to be wiretapped any more than I do.

My guess is siccing Reynolds on me was CeeCee's way of punishing me for deleting her computer's personal files. Hey, I know better than anyone that there is nothing more dangerous than a woman shorn of her famous apple pie recipe.

She'll survive.

In the meantime, Ryan has informed me that my employment is terminated. If anything, he's honest as to why. "Sorry Donna. Our biggest clients are POTUS, the CIA, the NSA, and the DOJ, in that order."

Realizing I'm in need of some TLC, Jack pulls me into his lap. "You can't just wallow away in a bottle of vodka. What do other ladies of leisure do?"

I laugh through my tears. "They do just that—wallow. Okay, maybe the libation of choice is vodka. Unless you mean I should make a pass at the neighborhood DILF."

"You've already won my heart."

"I've always appreciated your modesty."

"And I'm always in awe of your tenacity. Perhaps it's time you took up a hobby—something that matches your many excellent skill sets."

"That being, spycraft and assassinations?"

He sighs and pours a drink for himself—a double. "I was thinking more along the lines of baking, or crafts. You know, take time to have a little fun!" He thinks for a moment. "Here's an idea! Why not offer to plan Dominic's house-warming party for him?"

"Good thinking! If there's one thing I do well it's throw a stellar soirée. But Dominic isn't exactly talking to me these days."

Jack raises a brow. "Don't leave me in suspense."

"Truth is, I've been banned from Chateau Fleming because I … well, I broke in last week, and re-arranged the furniture."

Jack's brows come together, perplexed. "That's easy to

spin. You were, I don't know, testing his security system. And no doubt his bachelor pad could use a woman's touch."

"I thought so, too—in all thirty-four rooms, in fact." Yes, I am that bored. "But apparently my kindness left him somewhat disgruntled."

Seeing the look on Jack's face, I stutter, "Okay, maybe I lost something he was particularly enamored with—a life-size portrait of Princess Catherine! Did you know he still calls her 'Waity Katie?' Perhaps it's a good thing I've forgotten where I put it, considering that ship sailed long ago."

"I'll do what I can to work around it." He winces. "So that I'm fully prepared before I enter the lion's den, can you think of any other reason he may consider you *persona non grata*?"

I shrug. "And I guess he didn't like the fact that I changed the workout grotto into a real torture chamber. But hey, it's Dominic. As if listening to his jokes isn't torture enough, right? Other than that, I'm sure he'll come to his senses soon and realize I'm the right gal for the job."

Jack snaps his fingers. "Oh, by the way, Arnie found out that Penelope's volunteer wheel was in fact rigged."

"I knew it!" I slam my martini glass on the table.

"So, are you going to quit?"

"Heck no. Being the lunchroom lady is one of the few reasons I have to leave the house these days."

Jack frowns. "Since you're spending so much time at home, why not ingratiate yourself to Penelope and her coven by throwing a party here? After your gracious intervention with Cheever's election scandal, she needs another reason to hate you. Your party platters always get raves. Certainly that'll do the trick."

I hold both arms in front of me, palms up. "Let me see—" I lower the right one, just slightly. "I can make Penelope jealous —" I lower the left one, practically to my thigh. "Or I can exterminate a third-world dictator who orders the genocide of his country's indigenous people while he hits the poker tables in Vegas. A weighty dilemma if there ever was one."

"Okay, I'll admit it. Acme could have used your help in getting to that target. Ryan realizes it, too. But Donna, in this political climate—"

"Trust me, I get it, Jack. The president-elect is looking for any excuse necessary to cut Acme out of the picture."

"Ryan thinks it's a matter of biding our time." Jack has always been great at spin.

"Are you saying you're optimistic that I'll be able to shake the DOJ's surveillance sometime in the near future?"

He winces.

Thought so. We both know the reality of the situation: Catherine Connelly Martin may be running the country for eight years.

Ergo, I'm as good as retired.

"I wanted to walk away from this profession on my own terms, not those dictated by Catherine. She won't keep me from doing my job. I'm here to stay, and here to play," I declare loudly and proudly. "If need be, I will bide my time."

That alone is excuse enough for Jack to take another gulp,

this time straight from the bottle. Then he passes it to me, and I do the same.

What the hell. No one likes to drink alone.

I've just taken a swig when I notice Mary in the doorway. I hide the bottle behind my back as she knocks hesitantly on the doorframe. Yes, she saw me, but she's learned to cut me some slack. She's quite aware of my tender state over the past few months.

The good news is that she has been flourishing in school. In fact, all my children have. And I've been happy to hear from Babs' mother that her daughter is doing much better, too. Mary and Wendy have kept her close, reminding her, as only besties can, that they adore her.

The one joy I've had this winter was sharing with Mary some of my mother's recipes.

I beckon her forward with a smile. But my look changes to shock when she steps aside and we see Evan.

His eyes are dark and red-rimmed, as if he hasn't slept in days. I walk over to him and hold out my hand. "Evan, tell me—what has happened?"

He shakes his head. "I think my mother … I think my mother murdered my father." His declaration weighs so heavy on him that he bows his head. He pulls a thumb drive from his pocket. "The proof is here. I don't know what I should do with it, but I can't live with knowing that she'd do something like this, and get away with it."

Jack and I turn to each other. He nods at me, and I run into the family room.

Jeff is playing with my laptop. When I grab it out of his hands, he cries, "No fair!"

"This is a work tool, not a toy," I scold him.

He frowns. "But you haven't been working."

He doesn't need to remind me.

No matter. Something tells me that's about to change.

WHEN I RETURN WITH THE LAPTOP, I SEE JACK LOOKING OUT the window. "I don't see your Secret Service detail," he says to Evan.

Evan shrugs. "Mother is holed up out here, at Mr. Chiffray's, having strategy sessions with some money men. I walked through the front door of my school, handed the head of the school a fake note from my mother that said I was needed for some photo op, then I went out the back door with a friend. We caught the D.C. Metro to Dulles, and I hopped a plane here, using my friend's driver's license as identification. I put my airline ticket on his credit card, and paid him cash for it." He turns to me. "It's late enough that I guess everyone has figured out I'm gone and is panicking about now, but I had to get here, to you. When Dad realized he knew you back in high school, he told me that you were the most honest person he'd ever known. He said, 'I'm glad she's on our side.' It's the reason I'm here now. I had to share this with someone I could trust."

The lump in my throat hurts as I say, "I felt the same way about him. Tell me, Evan, what's happened?"

"Since Dad's death and then the election and all, my grades have slipped. I've had a hard time focusing on anything but … him." Evan glances away, ashamed. "The last thing my mom needs to hear is that I'm flunking trigonometry and physics. She's got too much on her mind, what with the inauguration next week." He frowns. "Unfortunately, last night I left my iPad at school, and they'd already locked it up for the night. Since my homework is in my iCloud account, I thought I'd sneak onto Mom's computer, access it there, then download it onto a thumb drive in order to move it onto my computer. She would have been angry, had she known. She's got a lot of confidential files on it—stuff that no one but members of the House are supposed to see."

"She's on the Intelligence, Foreign Affairs, and Energy committees as well as Armed Forces," I remind Jack

Evan nods first, then shakes his head. "You're right, but I swear, I never looked at any of those files. I just downloaded my homework and moved it onto a thumb drive I found on her desk. When I opened the thumb drive, I realized it also contained this video clip. It was taken from the security webcam at our Libertyville farmhouse. Here, let me show it to you."

He downloads the clip into my laptop.

The camera's point of view is the home's library. Catherine sits on the settee. A man sits on a chair, with his back to the camera. He wears a bulky coat, khaki pants, and a wide-brimmed fishing hat. His hands are gloved.

The man is Robert's shooter.

"I hear you're a crack shot," she says solemnly. "That you make no mistakes."

"I won't miss." The man assures her. He pauses then adds, "And don't worry, it'll be so quick that he won't suffer."

Once again, he's speaking through the voice changer software, but the cadence is the same.

In response, she closes her eyes and murmurs, "Good, yes. Painless."

She raises her hand to her face. Is she wiping away a tear? It's hard for me to tell because she drops her hand just as quickly.

"Afterward, you'll be a shoo-in." The man stands up, but all the while he keeps his back to the camera. "Isn't that what you want?"

She hesitates, then nods. "I just never thought I'd have to make … the ultimate sacrifice."

"Don't be so melodramatic, Congresswoman. You said it yourself—*he's standing in our way*. He didn't want you to run in the first place! Now look at you—your party's frontrunner! Well, almost. Who knew Randy Jennings would be last man standing against you? No one does 'stiff upper lip' like, you, lady. It's time to put it to good use; give the voters a reason to see your mettle in a time of adversity. That way, we all get what we want, including you—power, prestige, and a Swiss bank account filled with more money than you and your heirs can spend in six lifetimes."

She bites her lower lip, still not convinced.

"He's thinking of divorcing you."

"What?...You're—you're crazy!" Catherine's anger is tinged with doubt.

"Trust me, we've been monitoring his calls. He's already talked to one divorce attorney. If he follows through, you won't be able to get elected dogcatcher, let alone president."

She sits there for the longest moment. Finally, she nods.

The man disappears though the French doors leading to the garden.

Catherine turns toward the mantle. A framed photo of Robert catches her eye. She stares at it for a long time. Laughter can be heard. It's coming from another room. Robert's deep chuckle is echoed by Evan's belly laugh.

She lays the picture face down and sets a smile on her face before walking out the door, her head held high.

I turn off the tape then look up to see Evan's reaction.

His face looks set in stone. "We were laughing at some picture of Mom and Dad when they were in high school. When I saw the tears in her eyes, I thought she was sad because it reminded her of a time they were actually happy together. Now I know the truth." He looks up at me. "I'm not mistaken, am I? She knew what would happen to Dad, didn't she?"

I nod. "It was the same man, yes."

Tears roll down Evan's cheeks. "Then I've got to hand this over to the police. I didn't want to do it until I was sure."

"As it turns out, the Federal investigator who is in charge of the shooting is still in touch with me—sort of. Would you mind if we call him now, so that he can see it, too?"

Evan nods, as if in a trance.

Jack reaches for his cell phone. "Ryan, can you get Major Reynolds over here? We've got some evidence that may make a difference in his investigation … Yes, then we'll be expecting both of you."

The realization of what he's set in motion weighs so heavily on Evan that he collapses onto the couch. Mary sits beside him, cradling him in her arms. His life will never be the same. She knows this, too.

I want to hold my daughter; to tell her that love is stronger than hate or ambition or desire.

But Catherine has shown her the opposite.

Once again, Catherine proves she is unique: as a spouse, as a lover, and as a mother.

As for what she's done, and how she justified it to herself? It's just politics as usual.

19

Lame Duck

Someone holding public office whose term has expired or cannot be continued, and who therefore has less power to affect legislation than when his term started.

You may liken it to the power you have over your children, before they learn how to drive and can solo on their own. Once they have that driver's license, it's, "Mom Who?" and you're whistling in the wind created by them as they peel out of your driveway at breakneck speeds.

Speaking of the wind beneath wings, the lamest duck of all is one with a crispy-on-the-outside-but-tender-on-the-inside skin glazed in a delicious orange sauce, like so:

Honey-Dipped Duck (Adapted from AllRecipes)

Ingredients

- One Whole Duck
- Chopped Basil
- An Orange, quartered
- Teaspoon of Ginger Root
- 1 TSP Salt
- 1 Cup water
- 1 Cup Honey
- 1 Cup Orange Juice concentrate, thawed
- 1 TSP Lemon juice
- One stick Butter

Directions

1. Preheat oven to 350 degrees F (175 degrees C).
2. Mix the basil, ginger and salt in a small bowl, then sprinkle mixture on inside and outside of duck.
3. Stuff duck with orange quarters, and lay breast side up in roaster.
4. Add water to bottom of roaster.
5. In a small saucepan combine the honey, butter, lemon juice and orange juice concentrate. Simmer together over low heat until syrupy, then pour a little of the mixture over the duck, saving the rest for basting.
6. Cover roaster, and roast the duck in the preheated oven, for 30 minutes.
7. Turn duck breast down, reduce heat to 300 degrees F (150 degrees C) and roast, covered, for another 2 to 2 1/2 hours, or until very tender.

8. If desired, turn duck breast-up during last few minutes of cooking, to brown.

"HOW DARE YOUR DAUGHTER COERCE MY SON TO LEAVE HIS school!" Catherine's voice thunders through my house. "Ha! Figures that she'd turn out to be a conniving hussy, just like you."

Behind the shelf holding my good china is a secret compartment, which holds a SIG P22k DAK. While I am sorely tempted to flip the switch that accesses it, I temper my desire to do so with the knowledge that (a) the Secret Service detail assigned to Catherine would take me out quicker than my kitten heels will allow me to flee; (b) it's much better to keep Catherine alive, in order to get her to admit to her role in Robert's murder.

Unbeknownst to her, this little tête-à-tête is being watched and video-recorded by Ryan, Major Reynolds and Jack, from our panic room, which wasn't picked up in the Secret Service's threat assessment of my home.

In other words, I am the decoy that will make her a lame duck before she takes her first step into the Oval Office.

So yes, I keep my cool. "Catherine, Evan wasn't here to see Mary. He was here because of something he felt he should pass along to me. You see, like Robert, he trusts me more than he trusts you." I acknowledge her wince with a smile. "I felt you should see it first, since you've got the most to lose." I nod toward her Secret Service detail. "In private."

She hesitates. By now, she's used to living her life in the public spotlight. But she's still wary of sharing it with spooks who don't always take your secrets to the grave with them.

Finally, she motions them to leave us alone.

I wait a long moment after the door shuts behind them. Then I walk over to the coffee table and hit the button on my computer that starts the recording of her discussion with the assassin.

She gasps when she realizes what she's watching.

As each of the six and a half minutes ticks by, she doesn't say a word, but her face hardens with the realization that she can't hide behind a mask of ignorance, let alone one of innocence.

Finally the video stops, freezing on her heading out the door and to her fate.

"CeeCee, why did you do it—have Robert killed? Couldn't you have just run on your principles—or even your voting record?" I ponder that for a second then shake my head. "Sorry! I forgot who I'm talking to."

"I told you to never call me that," she says through gritted teeth. Seeing my frown, she calms down enough to wave away that pesky gnat of a thought. "He wanted a divorce! It would have ruined my chances of winning. Not to mention, he threatened to expose some of my most generous donors' less than worthy deeds." She shrugs. "It's easy to be a saint when you have no one to answer to."

I smile. "Well, you're lucky Evan came to me, who knew just what to do with it."

"Let's have it," she mutters.

"I beg your pardon?"

"Your ounce of flesh, my darling friend, Donna. Oh, quit acting so innocent! Obviously, you called me here because this is your bargaining chip." Ever in control, she sinks gracefully into an armchair. "Let's hear it."

"I wouldn't be so presumptuous." I bat my eyes.

She takes my broad hint that she should throw out the first bone. "I presume you want me to call off that mad dog, Major Reynolds. Such a pity! He was so perfect for the job, since he already has it out for you."

I roll my eyes in the hope that Reynolds is watching. *Toldja*, dude. "Yeah okay, that's a start. Keep it up, you're on a roll."

"I had earmarked the directorship of the CIA for someone else, but if promises aren't made to be broken in politics, then where, I ask you?"

"Oooh, the directorship—for *moi*?" I lay a hand on the cleft of my neck. "No thanks. I do better in the field. But I wouldn't mind having a few friends in high places."

"That could be arranged," Catherine says, almost too anxiously. She's losing her cool, poor thing. "Ryan Clancy, perhaps? Ah! Even better how about *your husband*?" She bares her teeth into a vicious smile that sends a chill down my spine.

I give my head a saucy shake. "He's not the desk jockey type, either."

She sighs as she walks over to my china cabinet and pretends to admire my dishes. They were my mother's pattern, in fact. Does she recognize them? I doubt it. "Here's a thought! Why don't I give you a diplomatic post? London, say—or Paris?"

I tilt my head, as if it would be a serious consideration, then shake my head. "That's a non-starter. Mary just started high school, and I wouldn't want to uproot her." I nod toward the screen. "Your assassin buddy seemed to think you were due for a big payday. Are you expecting the American people to vote for a presidential salary increase?"

"Ha! Are you kidding?" Her laugh now is less than infectious, almost guarded. "Everyone's got a little rainy day fund tucked away, right? I just happen to have mine far from prying eyes." She pulls open my silver drawer. Mother liked Francis I from Reed & Barton. I will pass it on to Mary. Catherine holds a knife up to the light to inspect its pattern. "If you're asking if I'd be willing to share, sure, why not? What will it take, Donna? A million? Two?"

"I'll let you know when the price is right." I walk over to her and put my hand on her shoulder. "You've put us both in an awkward position. Like last time, I'm not supporting your lie. I still can't fathom your thinking. Was it was worth knocking off Robert—your own husband, who loved you so dearly—for the glory of being our next president?"

"What do you know about us? About me? About the choices I've made, and why? Do I regret it? Of course I do! But sometimes … sometimes the means justify the end." She bows her head in shame.

She almost has me believing she feels some remorse,

except for the fact that she's admiring her supposedly grief-stricken profile in the mirror behind me.

She smiles at me through the mirror. "I presume your husband doesn't know about this little shakedown."

"Nope, just little ol' me. I'd rather he presume I'm his frugal little wifey."

"He'll make a handsome widower."

By the time the mirror reveals what she's holding behind her back, it's too late. She stabs me with a steak knife.

Thank goodness, it misses its mark—my gut—but it still catches me low, on my side.

I pull it out and stumble after her, but she's already out the side door.

What she doesn't expect is Rin Tin Tin and Lassie to side-swipe her on their way in to see if the kids dropped any dinner crumbs under the table.

Catherine's balance isn't helped when I pull the rug out from under her, literally.

The commotion she makes as she lands on her ass brings the Secret Service crashing through the door. Despite the blood gushing out of me, they tackle me and are about to cuff me when Jack, Ryan and Reynolds come bounding into the room.

Catherine doesn't get the fact that the jig is up. Instead, she stumbles through some silly scenario that has me attacking her with the knife while she wrestles it out of my hand and stabs me in self-defense.

I've got to hand it to the bitch—she's always the hero of her own story.

Reynolds explains to the Secret Service agents what just went down, and even puts the Attorney General on the phone, so that her detail gets the full lay of the land.

She is now their prisoner.

I turn to Reynolds. "Did you get what you needed?"

He nods, just as I pass out.

I wake to the sweet smell of roses.

Only one eyelid wishes to cooperate with my brain's mandate to open, and it does so only partially. Despite the cloud of fog around him, the man in the chair beside my hospital bed has all the right features to make my heart go pitter-patter. Even sitting, he towers over me. His hair is dark and thick. He must hear me stirring, because he makes the half-turn needed for our eyes to meet—

Lee Chiffray.

I bolt up, but before I topple out of the bed, he reaches over to steady me.

Even after he eases me back into a nest of pillows, his hand lingers in mine. It stays there until I shift my eyes toward the Secret Service agent whose head can be seen through my hospital door window.

He takes the hint, and leans back in his chair. "Your husband is picking up your children, but he should be back any moment now."

"Where's Babette?" My question comes out as a croak.

"She's with her stylist, shopping for the appropriate

outfit for our interview with Oprah. It takes place later tonight, at Lion's Lair"—he rolls his eyes—"after the news anchors school the American public on the little-used civics lesson as to why the vice president-elect can, and will, be sworn into the office of the presidency, instead of the candidate they voted for."

"That's disconcerting, to say the least. Considering it's the presidency, won't some sort of special election need to be held?"

He shakes his head. "No. Instead, the vice president assumes the role of president."

Without thinking, I pat my wound. Big mistake. Even the slightest touch elicits a wince. "I must have skipped that day in school."

"To put it simply, the Electoral College has already counted the votes and formally elected Catherine Connelly Martin as President of the United States. However, impeachment proceedings need not take place—that is, if she resigns prior to being sworn into office."

"The timing has worked out perfectly, hasn't it? The Inauguration is still a week away," I point out. "Still, I can't believe Catherine wouldn't be fighting this tooth and nail. If anyone knows how to spin a debacle, it's her."

"For once, Catherine has listened to reason. Even she knows it's for the good of the country that she resign immediately." He shrugs. "No one expects her to plead guilty, but the evidence against her is virtually insurmountable."

"Let me guess. She resigned on the condition that you commute her sentence before you leave office."

He laughs. "Smart lady! Go to the head of the class. Even if the voters grant me a second term, her appeals will still be meandering through the court system. I'll do it in my last hour as president."

"It is certainly a lucky turn of events for you, President-Elect Chiffray."

"If you say so. Frankly, the fact that the elected president will soon be a convicted killer means whoever sits in the Oval Office has a lot of work to do in regaining the nation's trust."

"You said that with just the right amount of humility and hope. You've certainly got your Oprah sound-bite down pat."

His smile wavers. "I've always loved the way you're able to laugh in the face of adversity." He picks up my hand again. This time, though, when I pull away, he doesn't let go. "You thought it right to bring Robert's killer to justice, no matter where the chips fell. Donna I want to thank you for that. He was a true friend to me." He looks down at my hand. "I've always felt you were my friend, too."

I don't know how to answer that. Despite Jack's grousing about him, his instincts are right. Since Lee and I met on Fantasy Island, it seems he's always in the wrong place at the right time.

Frankly, it's too uncanny to be coincidental.

"In fact, I hope you'll join Babette and me, as our guests, at the inauguration," he continues. "Consider the Lincoln bedroom reserved for you and … Carl."

His hesitation brings a blush to my cheeks. He's always

treated Jack politely, but coolly. "But surely you'll want to save that honor for some big supporter—"

"No, the honor is all yours. My God, you're the one who took a bullet—well, a knife—for trying to solve Robert's murder." He touches my side gently. "Besides, I've never had the need to take donations, so I owe nothing to anyone."

"It's good to hear you have no debts to pay off for being where fate has put you."

I meant that sincerely. So why does he look so sad?

Maybe it has something to do with the fact that Jack is staring at us through the hospital window.

"Ah, your loving spouse has arrived," he murmurs. "I'll leave you two lovebirds alone."

"Thanks for stopping by, Lee. I mean that, from the bottom of my heart." I wave Jack in. "Maybe he knows if Catherine has divulged the name of the shooter. I'm dying to know who it was. Professional curiosity, of course."

My declaration takes the smile off Lee's face. He nods curtly at Jack as he heads down the hospital hallway, with his Secret Service detail flanking him on all sides.

Jack looks from me to Lee and back again. "Talk about friends in high places. Mrs. Stone, you've certainly come up in the world."

"Make that 'we,' Tonto. We're now a power couple. And as such, guess where we'll be sleeping on the night of the inauguration?" I pat the bed.

He flops down beside me. "I'll be happy as long as it isn't here—or in jail."

I shift my body so that my head lies in the crook of his shoulder. "Neither. The Lincoln bedroom."

"Wow! Does that mean I have to wear a stovepipe hat?"

I raise a brow. "I'd prefer it if you didn't wear anything at all."

"You're on—that is, if you go commando, too."

I reward him with a pinky swear.

Then I let him peek under my hospital gown. He must like what he sees, because he's sporting an ear-to-ear smile. "Do you think the nurse will skip her rounds to your room if I put a sign on the door that says, 'If the hospital bed is rockin', don't come a'knockin'?"

I give him a kiss that suggests it's worth a try.

He's so happy that he's taking me up on it.

Now, if only the nurses would quit banging on the door.

20

Hail to the Chief!

Whenever the president makes a public appearance, the song played that announces him as he walks into the room is called "Hail to the Chief." It alerts all citizens, friends, family, voters and rubberneckers that, yes—the Chief Executive of our great nation has finally arrived!

Frankly, we should all have a song associated with us. For example, wouldn't it be great if Working in a Coalmine played over the intercom, whenever your boss stepped off the elevator? Or if the patter of your children's feet were accompanied by Baby Love?

And just imagine how great it would be if you knew your ex-husband was in shooting distance whenever you heard, I Still Miss You Baby, But My Aim's Gettin' Better.

One way you'll have them humming "Mmm Good," is with this recipe, which is fit for a White House reception:

Rose's Brisket (From Melissa Brown Zucker, Oceanside, New York)

Ingredients

- Thin-cut brisket, season to taste.
- 4 oz of stewed tomatoes
- Full can of water
- Bag of small red or Yukon Gold potatoes, peeled and quartered
- Carrots, sliced in ½-inch disks

Directions

1. Preheat oven to 350 degrees.
2. Season the brisket, to taste.
3. Add the tomatoes
4. Cover and put in oven for 1 1/2 hours.
5. Remove, slice meat, add peeled carrots and quartered potatoes.
6. Put back in oven for 1 1/2 hours.

Inauguration Day takes place on a frigidly cold and stormy day. Despite the initial shock and awe over Catherine's deed and the media circus surrounding her arrest and murder indictment, the crowd seems enthusiastic that a self-made tech baron is to be sworn in as the next President of the United States.

The American public's love affairs are fickle, and memories are short.

Babette insisted that we bring Trisha "to keep Janie company," quickly adding, "Don't worry! Hard to believe, but the West Wing has access to the best babysitters in the world." Not to mention a few Secret Service agents.

I'm looking forward to other such gems from Babette throughout Lee's presidency.

Admittedly, she kept it together when sitting knee-to-knee with Oprah on the celebrity interviewer's infamous sofa. By that I mean she sat silently, staring up adoringly at her husband while he did most of the talking.

In his inaugural speech, the crowd gets snippets of the same theme: how "the American people deserve the best government in the world. The amount they pay in taxes assures that." And that "Fate has put our paths together. On this journey, I will pilot you to safety, but only with the support and wise guidance of you, the American people, as my co-pilot. Your guidance will keep me on the right course."

However, the platitude that gets him the most applause, but concerns me to no end is the one that suggests, "The world we live in is a beautiful, wonderful place. But there are too many very dangerous people out there, who wish to take away our joys and our freedoms. We can't let them. We won't let them. Will we have to make sacrifices in order to stop them? Sadly, yes. But we will never sacrifice what we cherish most: our civil liberties."

This comes from a man whose primary business before the election was government contracts for data management and storage, as well as encryption and ciphering.

Two years from now, I'd like to take a peek at his blind trust. I'm sure it'll be an eye-opening experience.

WE'VE BEEN GIVEN TICKETS TO BOTH THE INAUGURAL BALL, and the Commander-in-Chief's Ball, to which Armed Forces personnel are invited.

The first one we hit is the CIC. Jack served in the Marine Corps, but I know he must feel strange holding a ticket that says, "Carl Stone," identifying him as a Navy Seal.

He's uncomfortable anyway. He still can't reconcile the series of events that led to a complete upheaval of the presidential race: the implosion of the frontrunners of both parties; Catherine's out-of-the-blue choice of Lee as her running mate; and the timing of her tragic downfall, leaving a total political novice as our Commander in Chief.

Considering the shenanigans in the elections that have come before it—such as the rumor that Chicago's first Mayor Daley stuffed the ballot boxes with votes from the dearly departed in Kennedy's election, not to mention the ignominious "hanging chad" ballots in GW Bush's first election—I'd say this one is the biggest head scratcher of them all.

If the GOP had run a closer race, maybe it would be

putting up a bigger fight. As it is, all is unusually quiet on the conservative front. I suppose that Lee's Stock Exchange cred has a lot to do with that. No one doubts he will be business-friendly. If anything it's the Dems who are waiting anxiously to see if their dark horse will show stripes that differentiate him from their herd.

In any case, I'm just happy waltzing around the room in Jack's arms. For just one evening, I want to forget that things aren't always as they seem.

When we come off the dance floor, he murmurs, "I guess I should rustle us up a couple of drinks from the bar." He's being gallant. I know he'd much rather hang out with some of his old Corps buddies, most of whom have made names for themselves within the heady corridors of the Pentagon.

I shake my head, and point to the table, where they've congregated … "Let me play barmaid. Go reminisce about your war stories with the other guys."

He pulls me in for a kiss.

When his lips are on mine, I know I'm home.

The closest bar is at the far end of the room. Unfortunately, the line winds halfway around the floor. Isn't there another bar around here? Ah yes, I remember where I saw it —on the mezzanine level.

I'd rather save my feet for dancing so, I make a beeline for the elevator.

When it opens, it's empty. The doors are about to shut when I hear someone call out, "Hold the elevator please."

The doors are already closing when I push the OPEN DOOR button. They hesitate, then part again—

I am facing *Carl.*

He's…alive?

And apparently still horny. Before I sidestep him and duck back through the closing elevator doors, he presses the button to the mezzanine with one hand, while shoving me against the back wall of the elevator with the other.

I open my mouth to protest, but he shoves his tongue down my throat.

So I bite down—hard. He howls in pain then slaps me—hard.

I taste blood, but I stand my ground, backhanding him with all my might.

His head snaps back with the force of my slap. Smiling, he lifts his hand to the red whelp that shadows his face. "You always did love it when I played rough."

I'm so shocked that all I can think about is to say the obvious. "But … back in Cabo, you fell into the bay! I thought you'd died!"

"You know what they say. What doesn't kill you only makes you stronger. I'm at the top of my game now, dear wifey, at everything. At hating. At wanting it all—especially you and my sweet little family." As one hand holds me against the wall by my shoulders, the other clutches my gown and inches up my leg. "You don't know how long I've waited to get you alone like this." Realizing that I've gone commando, he murmurs, "That's my girl. Nice! You don't know how long I've waited for this moment."

I don't think his fantasy included me kneeing him in the groin.

He groans as he doubles over. I run toward the elevator door and pound on it hard, but it won't open. Frantically, I smack every button in sight.

He straightens up and chuckles—hard to do when you're gasping for air. "Almost didn't recognize me, eh?" He strikes a bodybuilder's pose. "I'm broader in the shoulders. Can you tell? I tell you, Gitmo has a great workout facility. It's the only thing I miss about the joint. But I found a workout routine that will serve me for a lifetime."

"With the price on your head, you won't live long enough to find out."

"You're wrong. Since I've seen you last, I've taken out a couple of insurance policies."

"Such as?"

"For one, I ensured Catherine's nomination with a sympathetic nation."

Now I have the answer to my question. "You were Robert's shooter."

He laughs. "I was disappointed you didn't realize it at the time. That voice changer software is a technological marvel, don't you think?" He smiles. "You know how much it turns me on when you're so helpless. It was doubly sweet to find out he was your first love."

"You'll fry for what you did to him!"

"Nah. Don't think so." He turns to me. "Not now that my second insurance policy has kicked in."

"Oh yeah? What would that be?"

With the help of the elevator's mirrored door, he's able to

straighten his bowtie. "Take a wild guess who's being nominated as the Director of National Intelligence."

When I don't answer, he grins at me through the mirror. *"C'est moi, mon cher."*

I shake my head in disbelief. "But you're a terrorist—a fugitive from justice!"

"Not anymore. I was pardoned just this afternoon—by our new president." He nods proudly. "What are friends for, anyway?"

"Lee Chiffray … is your friend?"

"Why mince words? We're the best of bros! And I've promised him that there will be a lot of changes in how our spy networks will be run. For example, all the recent scandals with our black ops contractors will be a thing of the past because we're taking our business in-house. In fact, we'll be conducting a thorough audit of all contractor activities, to determine if any of them have been taking advantage of the country's goodwill. I wouldn't be at all surprised to find out that a contractor like, say, Acme, has been double-dealing with our enemies. Hey, here's a thought: maybe Acme made up the Quorum-you know, created a shadow organization, just to hang on the tit as long as possible. That's fraud, and that's jail time for our friend, Ryan—and of course Acme's agents, too. No one can say they were 'only following orders.'" He makes a Nazi salute. "In any event, it's goodbye Acme. How do you think Jack will fare in prison? Anyone who doesn't like your slick boyfriend could pay an inmate to bury a shiv where the sun don't shine."

Suddenly I feel ill.

"You look a bit queasy. Maybe you should put your head between your legs. Better yet, put it between mine. That'll make us both feel much better."

In his dreams. To make that point clear to him, I raise my knee to his groin again—

But he blocks it with his own knee, and the next thing I know he's slammed me up against the back elevator wall again.

He gazes down at me, as if I'm dessert. "You wouldn't dare," I growl.

"Who's going to stop me?" He laughs raucously. "Look at me, Ma! I'm king of the world! Your world, anyway, my little honeypot. And there's nothing you can do about it."

His lips loom down over mine—

But I'm saved by the bell.

As the elevator chimes our ascent onto the mezzanine level, a group of tipsy revelers bound in; Carl pulls me close and whispers in my ear, "Wish we had more time, my dear wife. But we'll soon meet again."

The thought roils my stomach.

When the doors open again on the first floor, I dart out between two barrel-chested sailors in full dress uniforms adorned with chest candy.

"Was it something I said?" Carl shouts out after me.

The elevator crowd laughs, as if the joke is on me.

Wait until they learn that it's on all of us—and it's far from funny.

"You look as if you've seen a ghost."

Jack presumes he's joking until I pull him aside and hiss, "I did—Carl. He's here."

Any joy Jack felt is now a thing of the past. He takes my hand and pulls me with him, out of the ballroom and into the lobby, so that we can hear each other over the band.

"Lee pardoned him, just this afternoon." I try not to be hysterical, but I feel cold panic surging through my veins. "Not only that, Lee is choosing him as the new director of the CIA."

"He can nominate the pope, if he wants. That doesn't mean the Senate Intelligence Committee is going to agree to let a known terrorist and assassin head up the CIA. Talk about a public relations disaster."

"You're right. It'll be interesting to see if Carl can leap that hurdle, and how Lee will help him do it." I hold his hand tightly. "And more to the point, you were right all along, about Lee Chiffray. Despite his squeaky clean paper trail, I guess he was Quorum all along."

He smiles. "A man always loves it when the woman he loves declares he's right, about anything, but talk about a pyrrhic victory."

Suddenly, I don't feel the urge to party. "Let's get the hell out of here."

"You mean, go to the White House?" He rolls his eyes. "Our gear is stowed in the Lincoln bedroom. Remember?"

"What? Not on your life. I don't want to be anywhere near Lee Chiffray! Let's grab Trisha and take the next plane home."

"The last flight left DC for the West Coast at least an hour ago. We'd have to wait until tomorrow."

"Then let's get a hotel room somewhere."

"With the Inauguration going on? That's impossible. Look Donna, I know the news that Carl is alive is upsetting, but he's not going to hurt us now—not if he truly wants to go straight. Let's just go on and live our lives." He takes my face between his hands. "And guess what? We've got the best room in town."

Hell yeah, we do.

I grab his hand and start for the coat room.

"What's your guess, did old Abe really sleep here?" Jack stares up at the Lincoln bedroom's ornate oval rosewood headboard that rises all the way to the ceiling. It is topped by a partial gold canopy, shaped like a crown. Its white lace sheers are draped in black velvet trimmed with old braid. The Lincoln bedroom's other elegant furnishings are also from the Victorian era.

Despite the embossed invitation, the private tour of the White House and the West Wing, and all of today's whirlwind of festivities, I still can't believe we're here, and for such a momentous occasion as a presidential inauguration.

To convince myself, I run my hand over the suite's wallpaper, a gold-white-and-red diamond pattern that mirrors a darker, larger pattern of the rug on the floor. "Mary Todd Lincoln chose the bed, but apparently he never slept in it—

although several other presidents have had the honor—not to mention some deep-pocketed presidential supporters."

A desk sits in the far corner of the room. On it sits a holographic copy of the Gettysburg address, signed by the man himself. In his own handwriting, I read the familiar words that every school child in the nation learns about and should never forget, considering the bloodshed that inspired the most famous presidential speech of all time:

… We here highly resolve that these dead shall not have died in vain — that this nation, under God, shall have a new birth of freedom — and that government of the people, by the people, for the people, shall not perish from the earth.

Every president since has kept this vow.

Now it's Lee Chiffray's turn.

One way or another, I plan on holding him to it.

Jack flops down on the bed. "I'm happy to report it doesn't sag." He pats the mattress. "Of course, with your help, we could give it a truly thorough road test."

I feign shock. "Aren't you afraid of Lincoln's ghost? At least twenty dignitaries and staff members have commented on it, so it's sure to show up while we make mad monkey love."

He shrugs. "I'm more afraid of our current live, dishonest president than I'd ever be of the spectral of Honest Abe."

"You're not the only one." I hop on the bed beside him. "Okay, I admit it, you were right."

He smirks. "As much as I love hearing that, which time are you referring to?"

"When we started this mission, you claimed my

woman's intuition was wrong about Lee. With both you and Chuck the Muckraker—not to mention the opposition party—having looked up his sphincter with a microscope and come up empty, I thought I was home free. But with Carl back from the dead, now we both know you were right."

"Glad you're willing to admit it." He stretches out on the bed. "I'd like my prize now, if you please."

"Really? And what would that be?"

He doesn't tell me. He opts to show me instead.

He pulls me down beside him. His kisses, on the back of my neck, start out light and sweet. But as they get deeper and more fervent, one hand outlines the curve of my ear, lingering on my lobe before inching down my neck. Finally it joins his other hand, which is slowly working the zipper of my dress down my spine.

Their diligence is rewarded when a plump breast lands in each hand.

He turns me around in order to take a long, sweet moment to admire them. From the look in his eye, I know he is tantalized by the decision before him: which peaked nipple should he tease first with his tongue?

He chooses the left, but readies the right one by tweaking it, oh so gently, between his thumb and forefinger.

I'm in heaven.

My anticipation to feel him inside of me keeps my hands busy, too. While one unclasps his belt buckle, the other nudges the button over his pants zipper to one side. Already he's grown rock solid.

Jack's groan is the cue I've been waiting for.

His eyes close as he shivers under my touch.

When they open again, the look he gives me speaks volumes. It warns me that he will now take control, and that what will follow will bring me joy, even as it brings me to tears.

I will plead with him to stop, and beg for more.

I will curse him for breaking me down, and bless him for loving me so completely.

Then I will do the same to him.

We've both learned that the best way to deal with the ghosts who haunt us is to face them, and put them to rest, once and for all.

Carl doesn't have a chance in hell.

—THE END—

Next Up for Donna!

The Housewife Assassin's Hollywood Scream Play

(Book 7)

Lights, cameras and non-stop action! When Donna and Jack are placed on Interpol's Most Wanted list, they go on the lam by accepting an offer to act as espionage experts on a movie set.

Other Books by Josie Brown

The True Hollywood Lies Series

Hollywood Hunk

Hollywood Whore

The Totlandia Series

The Onesies - Book 1 (Fall)

The Onesies - Book 2 (Winter)

The Onesies - Book 3 (Spring)

The Onesies - Book 4 (Summer)

The Twosies - Book 5 (Fall)

The Twosies – Book 6 (Winter)

The Twosies - Book 7 (Spring)

The Twosies - Book 8 (Summer)

More Josie Brown Novels

The Candidate

Secret Lives of Husbands and Wives

The Baby Planner

How to Reach Josie

To write Josie, go to:
mailfromjosie@gmail.com

To find out more about Josie, or to get on her eLetter list for
book launch announcements, go to her website:
www.JosieBrown.com

You can also find her at:

www.AuthorProvocateur.com

twitter.com/JosieBrownCA

facebook.com/josiebrownauthor

pinterest.com/josiebrownca

instagram.com/josiebrownnovels